ONE

Becca Price's slowly healing back shouted its discomfort as she heaved the water hose into the horse's stall to fill the bucket. She ignored the pain and listened to the old barn creak. The feeling of someone watching her spiked the hairs on her neck and she shuddered.

Someone watching, waiting. Not exactly how she wanted to start her Monday morning.

The ominous feeling had just grown stronger over the past few weeks ever since her fall. She glanced around and did her best to shake off the creepiness.

Again.

Unfortunately, she just couldn't quite manage it. A shiver rippled up her spine and it had nothing to do with the forty-degree temperatures outside.

"Nathan? Is that you?" Nathan Williams, her former best friend and reformed practical joker, was back in town and asking to see her. Maybe he'd come early and was reverting to their teenage days.

Silence echoed back at her. She wished Jack, her five-year-old golden retriever, had followed her into the barn. He'd tell her if someone was out there. But he'd taken off across the backyard and through the pasture.

She shook her head. "Focus on the horses," she

muttered. Owning her own barn had been a dream since childhood. A little pain—and paranoia—wouldn't stop her from giving her clients what they'd paid for. "One down, eleven more to go."

She moved to the next stall. The pretty paint nickered and nuzzled up against Becca's face. Absently, she stroked the animal's warm neck. She couldn't help but scan the open area between the stalls once more, even as she took comfort in the horse's calming presence. He didn't seem worried. Becca stepped back and her foot caught the edge of the bucket, dumping what she'd just filled.

She sighed and righted the pail to start over. Even with all of the hard work, she wouldn't do anything else, have any other career—not even use the medical degree she'd been arm-twisted into getting. At least, not right now. Right now, horses were her passion.

No matter the backlash she got.

Becca tightened her jaw. She'd succeed. She *would*. She'd find the money to keep the barn going. Somehow, someway. And she *wouldn't* ask her parents for help—that was for sure. She'd go back to working a full-time job before she'd ask them for help. Which they wouldn't give her anyway.

Don't let me give up, please God. Give me strength. The prayer felt weird, and she felt almost guilty for praying it. Her parents had both been born in Wrangler's Corner and grown up not too far from where Becca now lived. But they'd had bigger dreams than horses and ranching. Not only for themselves, but for her, too. Their only child. So they'd packed her up and moved to Nashville when she was seventeen years old.

She still wasn't sure she'd forgiven them for that—

The white truck drew closer.

Becca pressed the gas pedal then let off. She'd let the truck go around her if he was in that much of a hurry. She slowed. He closed in fast. Too late, she realized he wasn't going to pass her. Instead, he rammed the back of her truck.

Becca cried out and spun the wheel to keep the vehicle on the road. Another slam sent her into a spin. She screamed and stepped on the brakes. Her truck slowed, but the pedal felt squishy and then went to the floor.

In horror, she realized she was headed straight for the side of the mountain. Becca spun the wheel one more time and managed to keep from going over, but it put her face-to-face with the person trying to kill her.

He gunned the engine of his vehicle and Becca slammed hers into Reverse then hit the gas. She lurched backward, and the attacker flew past her.

Becca hit the brakes, and this time the pedal didn't even pause as it slammed against the floor.

She continued to move backward and dropped over the edge of the mountain road.

Lynette Eason and her daughter, **Lauryn Eason**, teamed up to write *Christmas Ranch Rescue* after Lauryn made it to the final round in the 2014 Love Inspired Suspense Killer Voices contest. Lauryn is now a sophomore in college and plans to major in international studies and communications. Lynette is the bestselling, award-winning author of almost forty books. She writes for Revell and Harlequin's Love Inspired Suspense line and can be found online at www.lynetteeason.com.

Books by Lynette Eason

Love Inspired Suspense

Classified K-9 Unit
Bounty Hunter

Wrangler's Corner
The Lawman Returns
Rodeo Rescuer
Protecting Her Daughter
Classified Christmas Mission
Christmas Ranch Rescue

Family Reunions
Hide and Seek
Christmas Cover-Up
Her Stolen Past

Rose Mountain Refuge
Agent Undercover
Holiday Hideout
Danger on the Mountain

Visit the Author Profile page at Harlequin.com for more titles.

CHRISTMAS RANCH RESCUE

LYNETTE EASON
LAURYN EASON

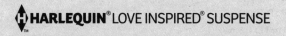

LOVE INSPIRED BOOKS

ISBN-13: 978-0-373-45747-2

Christmas Ranch Rescue

Copyright © 2017 by Lynette Eason and Lauryn Eason

All rights reserved. Except for use in any review, the reproduction or utilization of this work in whole or in part in any form by any electronic, mechanical or other means, now known or hereinafter invented, including xerography, photocopying and recording, or in any information storage or retrieval system, is forbidden without the written permission of the editorial office, Love Inspired Books, 195 Broadway, New York, NY 10007 U.S.A.

This is a work of fiction. Names, characters, places and incidents are either the product of the author's imagination or are used fictitiously, and any resemblance to actual persons, living or dead, business establishments, events or locales is entirely coincidental.

This edition published by arrangement with Love Inspired Books.

® and TM are trademarks of Love Inspired Books, used under license. Trademarks indicated with ® are registered in the United States Patent and Trademark Office, the Canadian Intellectual Property Office and in other countries.

www.Harlequin.com

Printed in U.S.A.

Whoever dwells in the shelter of the Most High will rest in the shadow of the Almighty. I will say of the Lord, "He is my refuge and my fortress, my God, in whom I trust."

–Psalms 91:1-2

To the amazingly smart, supercute,
sweetest little three-year-olds ever, Lynette's niece and
nephew and Lauryn's cousins, Shelby Elizabeth and
Thomas Lane. We love you to the moon and back
and pray you grow up to realize how wonderful
our crazy family is in spite of all our imperfections.

even though she'd gone along with it without outward argument.

Somehow she'd survived the move, the new school, and the never-ending social engagements she'd been required to attend. She'd excelled at pleasing her parents.

Until she'd had enough.

A year ago, she'd bought this place with the small bit of money her grandmother had bequeathed her and moved home.

The barn door squeaked again and she jumped. "Nathan? If that's you, it's not funny."

Silence echoed back at her. Nathan used to like practical jokes, was always pulling off some stunt when they were in high school, but he'd never been mean or deliberately creepy. Even he wouldn't take it this far. When he'd called this morning and asked to see her, she'd been stunned. Pleasantly stunned for sure, but she knew she hadn't hidden her surprise well. "I'm back in town," he'd said, "and I need some work. Do you think I could come talk to you about a job?"

She stumbled through a *yes* and he'd promised to be there shortly.

But even he couldn't have gotten here that fast. So that meant someone else was there. But who and why wouldn't that person answer her?

Her pulse began a swift beat and her nerves shivered. Becca kinked the hose and the water flow stopped. She stepped from the stall and looked out into the open area. Nothing. Again. She shuddered and bit her lip, chastising herself for jumping at her shadow. No one was there after all.

The door to the barn creaked but didn't open. She stomped her foot and turned back to stare at the door.

She'd moved too fast. Pain shot through her and she grimaced. "Hello?"

Only the sounds of the horses answered her. Her nerves stretched and she moved from the stall to the center of the barn. Her boots crunched on the combination of dirt and scattered hay as she stopped and listened. Before the accident, she would have marched up to the door and thrown it open. Now, fear invaded her body, and she shivered. It didn't make sense, but she couldn't shrug it away.

She reached for the pitchfork she'd leaned against the stall opposite the paint's.

A flash of memory taunted her. Pounding hooves and a horse's crazed whinny. She gasped and knew the memory was from the day of her fall. She had very little recollection of what had happened that day.

Four weeks ago, when she'd awakened in the middle of the field, the pain had taken her breath away. Christine Hampton, her trainer, had been on the phone screaming at the 911 dispatcher.

Now it seemed as if someone was trying to get in her barn. And Becca didn't know if she had the strength to defend herself if that someone had evil on his mind.

Nathan Williams watched the trees pass by as his anger simmered beneath the surface. The conversation with Clay Starke had riled him, and he almost missed the turn for Becca Price's gravel drive. He pressed the brake hard and made a quick turn in the right direction.

Once he knew he was back on track, he let the conversation he'd had not twenty minutes earlier run through his head. He'd been in Clay's office, sitting across from the man who'd just asked him to spy on the woman who'd been his best friend since childhood.

Granted, they hadn't spoken much in the past several years, but she'd meant the world to him once upon a time, and he was kicking himself over what he'd just agreed to do.

When Clay Starke, sheriff in the small town of Wrangler's Corner, Tennessee, located about an hour outside of Nashville, had called asking for his help, Nathan had listened with the intention of letting Clay down gently.

However, when his friend had told him about Becca's accident and that she was desperate for help, he hadn't been able to say no. He'd come home and found out what was really going through Clay's mind. "It's possible she's running drugs off her ranch and I need it proven one way or another."

"There's no way that's possible." He'd immediately defended Becca. "I'm not going to do it." He'd shoved the chair back and stood, anger thumping through him. Betrayal burned in his belly. "You lied to me."

Clay had leaned forward, regret and determination stamped on his lined face. "I didn't lie. I just didn't tell you everything because I knew this would be your reaction. I remember how crazy you were about Becca in high school."

"Yeah, well, she wouldn't give me the time of day, so it doesn't really matter, does it?" At least not in the romance department. But she'd loved hanging out with him at his house and playing Sunday afternoon football in the big backyard with him and his dad.

Clay had sighed and rubbed his eyes. "I'm at the end of my rope, Nate. People are dying. The last victim of an overdose, Donny Torres, was only nineteen years old. And while he had a rap sheet as long as your arm, he didn't deserve to die."

"I agree."

"I talked to Donny's parents. I've known them for a while now, and I knew Donny well. He was a hard case, I'll admit. He didn't hang around with the good guys, and his name has popped up several times in my various investigations. I think he knew a lot more about the drugs in this town than he was letting on. And…"

"And?"

"He had Becca's cell phone number in his phone. When I asked her who he was and why he would have her number indicating a call from her, she said she didn't know. I mean, she knew Donny, of course, it's a small town. But she said she had no idea why he had her number in his phone and that she'd never called him."

"Maybe she didn't."

"I pulled her records and they had a ten-minute conversation the day of her accident. Two days before that, they talked for six minutes, and a week before that, they talked for four and a half minutes. And there was a text message to him that said, 'Shipment 125 4AM.'"

Nathan had frowned. Okay, that was kind of weird. "What did she say when you told her you had a record of the calls and the text?"

"She just shook her head and denied knowing anything about them. And honestly, she did look completely confused. But…I don't know, Nate, I just don't know. You and I've worked the bigger city crimes. You know what good actors some people are. My gut is saying she's innocent, and my heart wants to agree, but the evidence is saying otherwise."

"Did you get a warrant to search her place?"

Clay had grimaced. "Yes. Last week. I thought the message about the shipment might mean December 5, at four in the morning. I staked the place out that night and never saw a sign of anyone. But I'd already put off the search as long as I ethically could, so I had no choice but to go in. Rumors were swirling, and people were demanding something be done—especially Donny's parents. I can't say I blame them."

"And?"

"And, I'm happy to say, we found nothing."

"Did you use a drug dog?"

"Yes. I had a buddy bring one in from Nashville. The dog got a little antsy in the barn but never alerted to anything. We searched the barn anyway. Tore the place apart and still found nothing."

"Then…could someone have it out for her and be trying to set her up?"

"Of course it's possible, but again, I just don't know. I mean, if someone was going to set her up, I would think we would have found something, not come away empty-handed."

"Yeah. True."

"I do know she's hurting for money, and sometimes desperate people do desperate things."

"Hurting for money?" Nathan had raised a brow. "With her parents? That's not how I remember things. Her parents are loaded."

"Becca and my aunt and uncle had a falling-out when she quit her job at the hospital and moved back to Wrangler's Corner. I'm not sure they've spoken over the last year."

"Whoa."

"Yeah." Clay had sighed and raked a hand through his dark hair. "Look. Whoever's running these drugs through my town has to be stopped. If it's Becca, then so be it. I need you to do this because I can't be objective."

"And you think I can?"

"You have to." He'd pierced him with a hard look. "High school was a long time ago. You've moved on. You were engaged to another woman, which means you were over Becca."

That was true. And, had he married Sylvia, he wouldn't have thought twice about Becca. But Sylvia's betrayal had shifted something inside of him. Made him long for the innocence and sweetness that had encompassed his relationship with Becca. He'd liked being with her, had respected her and, yes, wanted more than friendship, but knew she hadn't, so he'd been content just to hang out with her. Until she moved.

He realized Clay was waiting for him to respond. "Yes, I was over Becca. What I felt for her was a teenage crush. And, yes, I truly loved Sylvia." Which was why her betrayal had nearly gutted him. "But—"

"No buts. You need to keep your feelings out of it. She's off-limits until we know for sure she's not involved."

The shock of Clay's omission about Becca's suspected involvement had faded, leaving a simmering anger. Nathan had jabbed a finger at the man he'd always looked up to and trusted. "You said you needed my help. You said there was a drug ring operating right under your nose. And you *said* that Becca was hurt and I could work for her while I decided whether or not I wanted to go back with the DEA. You just said you wanted me to *investigate*. You didn't say anything about going undercover or suspecting that Becca was involved in the drug running."

"Nath—"

"You want me to lie to her and I won't do it." He'd ended his tirade and rubbed his left shoulder, the ache a constant reminder of why women were off-limits.

Especially Becca.

He'd once thought himself in love with her, a middle school crush that had grown as they'd moved into their teenage years. But he'd gotten over her and moved on.

Or so he'd thought.

The feelings that had raced through him once he realized the intent behind Clay's manipulation made him understand he'd been fooling himself. And that made him mad. He had no intention of fanning an old flame, but the desire to see Becca and protect her from whatever was going on unsettled him. Sylvia had taught him that romance was a waste of time and should be avoided at all costs.

And yet…Becca would never do what Sylvia did.

Would she?

He hated the small kernel of doubt that sprouted its ugly head, but he couldn't help it. People changed, he knew that. But was it possible for Becca to change that much?

For the most part, Nathan had physically healed from the gunshot wound to his shoulder, but emotionally healed was another story.

After he had refused to budge on his insistence that Clay was wrong and he'd have no part of the scheme, the man had finally said, "Then prove she's innocent."

Those four words were why he'd called her and asked to see her, and why he now found himself in Becca's driveway, fingers still clamped around the wheel of his pickup truck.

A hand slapped over her mouth and jerked her head back. Pain assaulted her and Becca let out a squeal as the pitchfork slid from her fingers to bounce on the dirt.

Jack, her golden retriever, bounded into the barn, barking and lunging at the man behind her.

"Shut up!" He danced sideways to avoid Jack's snapping jaws, keeping Becca between him and the dog.

Becca struggled, her back screaming in protest at the rough treatment. She finally managed to jam an elbow into his torso. He gave a low grunt and his hand slipped enough for her to open her mouth and bite down.

Yelling, he shoved her away from him. Becca kept her feet beneath her and stumbled for the door while her back spasmed and her head spun. Then the pain overwhelmed her and sent her to her knees. She cried out, unable to do anything except pray her attacker was done.

"Hey! What's going on in here?"

Jack continued his frantic barks, but she knew the voice that had come from behind her. She rolled, gasping at the arch of fire that burned up her back.

Her attacker had grabbed the pitchfork and was headed toward her friend. "Nathan, watch out!"

With the black ski mask covering his features, she had no way of knowing who he was, just that he was getting ready to stab Nathan.

Nathan waited until the man almost reached him, then spun and kicked out, giving a grunt of satisfaction when his foot connected. The pitchfork flew from the attacker's hands.

The masked man lunged for the door. Nathan let him go and raced to Becca's side. He dropped to his knees. "Becca, are you okay?"

"I'll live," she gasped. "Don't let him get away." Jack ran after the escaping intruder. "No! Jack, come!" The dog stopped and returned to Becca. He paced in front of her, his concerned brown eyes never leaving her face.

Nathan's blue eyes snapped to the barn's exit, then back to her. "I'm more concerned about getting you to a doctor, but stay put. I'm going to check on him and call 911."

She nodded and closed her eyes, nausea sweeping over her. Residue from the pain and fear, she was sure.

"I'll be right back, I promise. Just going to try and get him."

Nathan raced away from her and she tried to roll to her side. The lightning flash of pain that swept through her stopped that idea. She lay still, swallowing, doing her best not to be sick. Desperation and fury washed through her. She'd reinjured her back. All the therapy and exercises and taking it easy had been undone in the blink of an eye. If she got her hands on the person responsible—

"He's gone," Nathan said, coming back into the barn. "He had a car stashed out of sight, backed into the woodsy part near the top of your drive. I would have chased him but didn't want to leave you here alone and hurt." He held out a hand. "Can I help you up or would you rather wait for the ambulance to get here?"

She stared up at him, considering her options. "I think as long as I don't move, I might manage to keep from hurling."

He squatted, his jeans pulling tight against the muscles in his legs. His boots had seen better days and the cowboy hat hid his eyes. She reached up and flicked it off. His blue eyes set in his permanently tanned face stared down at her. He blinked and then smiled. "You haven't changed."

"Neither have you." She took a deep breath and moved slowly. Her back muscles twinged but didn't lock up on her. She held up a hand. "I'll take a little help if you can pull nice and easy so I don't have to use my back."

He did. Pretending she had a metal rod in place of her spine, she got to her feet. No bending, no moving fast, no twisting. Her head beat a fast rhythm of pain along with the throbbing in her back. "Thanks."

Jack whined and nudged the side of her leg. She absently gave his ears a scratch, and that seemed to pacify him.

Sirens filled the air around them. She took a deep breath and a step forward. It hurt, but at least it didn't feel like she had a knife wedged in her back anymore.

"You need to get to a doctor and have that checked out."

She didn't bother telling him she *was* a doctor. He knew that. Not a back doctor, true, but… "I know what's wrong and I know how to fix it. Rest and physical therapy." She grimaced. "Neither of which I like very much."

"I'm thinking a pain pill wouldn't hurt."

She tightened her jaw. "I don't do drugs—in spite of what everyone in Wrangler's Corner thinks."

He lifted an eyebrow and studied her. "I wasn't suggesting you did. I saw Clay earlier and he told me you had a serious back injury."

"I do. Did. It's in the healing process. Or it was before just now." She'd done the narcotics in the beginning, just to get through the day, but fearing addiction, she'd weaned herself off, and before the attack, had been at the point where she could just take something over the counter when she needed it. Like when she overdid it. Although she had to admit, the pain now was bad enough to have her thinking twice about finding her prescription bottle.

Nathan hovered at her side. "I'm glad I showed up when you did," she said to him.

"I'm glad I did, too."

She tilted her head. "Why do you need a job? I thought you were some big bad DEA agent in Nashville."

His eyes shuttered and his jaw tightened. "I am. Was. Am. Not the big and bad part. Just the agent part."

"So which is it? Am or was?"

"Was. I quit." He pursed his lips and ran a hand through his hair. "Actually, it's more like an extended leave of absence, but I have an open invitation to return anytime." He sighed. "I got shot and decided to come home to recover. I have more time off than I need, I'm just not ready to—" He stopped and shook his head. "I'm healing nicely and boredom has set in." He gave a small shrug. "I heard you needed help, I've got some medical bills to pay, so I'm here to apply."

He'd been shot? How had she missed hearing about that one? No doubt because she lived like a hermit most of the time. She looked him over carefully. "You don't look hurt."

"It wasn't a bad wound, and like I said, I'm healing. Actually, the shoulder is pretty much healed. I've done the physical therapy and I'm cleared to go back to work. I just don't want to yet." His eyes darkened and he glanced away. "Besides, hurt comes in many different forms," he murmured.

Two Wrangler's Corner police vehicles pulled to a stop in her drive, and she walked toward them, keeping her pace even, careful with each step. She recognized Trent Haywood and Parker Little. A third car pulled in behind them. Clay.

Clay stepped out of the third car and Becca kept her

gaze on the man. *Hurt comes in many different forms.*
Well, that was true enough.

Sheriff Clay Starke was her cousin. The one she'd
chased around his parents' ranch when they were kids,
and the one who'd beat up the bully for her when she
was in second grade. He was also the one who'd questioned her about a man who'd died of an overdose with
her number in his cell phone and who'd gotten a warrant to search her place. Thankfully, as she'd expected,
he'd come up empty-handed.

But still.

The anger and hurt were fresh and she didn't know
when she'd get over it. She glanced back at Nathan.
"You're hired."

He blinked. "That was easy."

"I need help and you want to work. I know you and I
trust you. I was going to have to put an ad in the paper
and start interviewing." She grimaced. "I want to do
that about as much as I want another fall. I'd be a fool
to turn you down."

I know you and I trust you.

Nathan stared at the bottom of the bunk above him,
his mind spinning, guilt eating at him. Becca thought
she knew him. She *thought* she could trust him. Little
did she know she'd just let a spy into her midst. She
knew he worked for the DEA and yet hadn't thought
twice about letting him onto her property or hiring him.
That spoke volumes to him.

He grunted and rolled to his side, winced at the pressure on his shoulder and decided he was most comfortable on his back. *God, I think I've managed to get myself
into a mess. Please don't let me do anything that's going
to hurt Becca. I wouldn't hurt her for the world, but*

Clay's asked me to do this. And while I don't think Becca's guilty, if Clay says the drugs are coming from this area, then I need to find out. And find out if Becca's gotten mixed up in the middle and doesn't know it. He sighed. "Although, I'm guessing she might know it after today," he muttered aloud. It had been a bold move for the masked man to attack her in the barn in the middle of the day. That very fact scared him. For her.

Which made him wonder if the failure to get what he wanted would result in the attacker's return.

Nathan slapped the pillow in frustration. Sleep wasn't going to happen. His nerves still jumped from his showdown with the man in the barn, his worry over Becca, and his desire to tell her exactly what he was doing sleeping in her bunkhouse and working at her barn.

He swung his feet to the floor and grabbed his jeans from the foot of the bed. So he'd tell her. Right now. Nathan glanced at the clock and winced. It was shortly before midnight. He'd have to wait until morning. She'd had a long day and needed her sleep. "And so do you, Williams," he muttered. "Lights out."

Nathan wasn't sure how long he laid there, thinking, running different versions of a confession to Becca about his presence through his mind, but when the floorboard creaked, his eyes popped open. He lay still, barely breathing, not moving.

Another soft creak, the thud of a footfall. Someone was in the bunkhouse. But who? And why? It wouldn't be Becca, she would have texted or called to let him know she was coming down.

Had her attacker returned after all?

Nathan sat up and reached for his gun.

TWO

Becca checked the clock once more and sighed. Midnight. She couldn't get her nerves to calm down long enough to let sleep take over, which was why she now sat in the dark kitchen sipping hot decaf tea and looking out over her property. Jack lay on the floor at her feet, his presence a comfort.

The half-moon cast a faint glow and shadows danced in the distance. But at least the pain in her back had eased and she was able to move without the constant ache. Apparently, her attacker hadn't done as much damage as she'd feared and she'd bounced back quickly. She just wished her brain could do the same. Unfortunately, the attack kept playing over and over in her restless mind.

Becca shivered and pulled the blanket she'd snagged from the den tighter around her shoulders.

Was he out there? She sipped the tea and took comfort in the fact that her Winchester .45 leaned against the wall nearby.

She still had a hard time processing that she'd been attacked. On her property, in her barn.

Anger mingled with remembered fear. She'd never

felt afraid in her home before and now she jumped at every familiar noise.

The moment she'd heard the Updikes were selling the property, she'd known what she'd wanted to do. Her parents had balked. She'd been an equestrian champion as a teen, then graduated at the top of her class from medical school.

On the fast track to following in her father's impressive footsteps, she was supposed to become a surgeon just like him and continue making them proud while giving them bragging rights at all of their snobby social functions. Well, her father anyway. Her mother hadn't been quite as vocal—and wasn't nearly as snobby.

And while Becca loved medicine and the thrill of helping someone heal, she'd also had other dreams.

Like a stable of her own. Riding lessons and trail rides. The squeal of children's laughter. When she'd finally had the guts—and the means thanks to her grandmother—to chase those dreams, she'd done it. And since her father had paid all of her medical school bills, she'd had no debt to tie her down initially. She'd set up a stable, took advantage of the fact that she knew everyone in the equestrian business and built her clientele so fast it made her head spin.

However, she had to admit, her favorite part was her special needs riders. No amount of money, no ribbon or trophy gave her the satisfaction like seeing a child's eyes light up while on the back of a horse.

Her eyes grew heavy and she drained the last of the tea from her cup. As she rose to carry it to the sink, a flash of light caught her attention. It came from the bunkhouse. Probably Nathan being as antsy as she. But she couldn't help the sliver of uneasiness that inched its way up her spine.

Jack lifted his head, his ears perking, his attention on the door.

What if her attacker had come back? What if he decided to incapacitate Nathan while he slept and then came to find her? She tightened her jaw and went to slip her feet into the boots she'd left by the back door, being careful not to jar her back. "Come on, Jack, let's see what's going on." Grabbing the rifle, she slipped out into the chill of the night with the dog at her heels.

Nathan had lost track of how long he'd stayed quiet, his fingers curled around the grip of his weapon. He kept his back to the wall, eyes on the door in front of him. The floor had creaked a couple more times, then silence. In spite of his pulse pounding and his adrenaline rushing, his senses were sharp, focused.

If Becca's attacker had returned, Nathan was determined to make sure he didn't get another chance at her. Although why would he come into the bunkhouse if he was after Becca?

Nathan moved to the door, his socked feet silent on the hardwood. He had a momentary memory blip of the crack house he'd helped bust two months ago and his breath caught. It had been a setup. They'd known he and his team were coming thanks to Sylvia's betrayal. The only reason Sylvia and the others had been there was because the team had moved their timetable up three hours.

But the drug dealer had been prepared with a full arsenal of weapons and people to use them.

The bullet had come out of nowhere, catching him in the shoulder. He'd gone down in a blinding flash of pain and awareness that if he didn't do something, he was dead.

Nathan swallowed against the memories. His blood roared in his ears as he planted his back against the wall and closed his eyes. He ordered his heart to slow while he focused on the present. Right now, he needed to figure out who was making the floors creak. The Glock felt comfortable in his grip.

A grunt and a sigh reached his ears. Nathan frowned. Not the noises of someone trying to be quiet. He stepped into the short hallway, grateful for the dim glow from the night light plugged into the outlet. He tried to stay in the shadows but knew if someone looked down the hall, at the very least, they'd see his profile.

The bunkhouse was fairly large, probably about a thousand square feet total. Three small bedrooms, two bathrooms, a kitchen and living area. He'd chosen the bedroom nearest the front door. The noises had come from the bedroom to his left. Nathan slipped down the hall, alert for any movement. A flashlight beam bounced off the wall to his right. It came from the bedroom where he'd heard the noises.

"Who's there?" he called out, then moved into the bathroom located in between the bedrooms in case someone decided to shoot for his answer. Everything stilled. "Answer me."

Light footsteps from inside the bedroom reached his ears. He hefted the weapon and aimed it at the door.

Which someone pushed closed. Nathan stared.

At the other end of the bunkhouse, the front door shut with a quiet snick. So quiet he almost wondered if he'd heard it. But knew he had.

He spun to face this next threat, his gaze bouncing between the entrance to the hall and the bedroom with the closed door. Light footsteps fell softly on the hardwood. He moved from the safety of the bathroom and into the hall that led to the large living area and the front door. He peered around the edge and saw a dark shadow moving across the floor toward him. He swung his weapon up. "Freeze."

Becca froze. "Nathan?"

"Becca?" His arm lowered the weapon away from her. His shoulders relaxed a fraction in the dim light.

"What's wrong?" she whispered. Jack bounded up beside her and she placed a hand on his head. "Jack, shh!" He settled at her side.

"Someone's in the room at the end of the hall," Nathan said.

"Who?"

"I don't know. I was getting ready to find out when I heard you sneak in. Why didn't you knock?"

"I saw lights flickering and thought I saw someone sneaking around the bunkhouse. I wanted to make sure you were all right without letting whoever was here know that I saw him."

They kept their voices low as they moved toward the hallway that would take them to the back bedroom. Nathan stopped. "Stay here," he whispered.

"No way."

"If someone starts shooting, I don't want you in the way."

She hefted the rifle in her right hand. "Thanks, but I know how to take care of myself. Let's figure this out together."

She thought she heard, "Stubborn woman," before he moved to the door and stood to the side. He lifted his hand and rapped his knuckles on the wood. "Open up and come out! Keep your hands where I can see them."

Silence.

Becca frowned. Who could be in there? Why would her attacker go in the bedroom and shut the door?

The mental light went on. "Wait a minute," she whispered. "I know who's in there."

"Who?"

"Brody MacDougal. We call him Brody Mac."

"Who's that?"

"One of my lesson students turned volunteer turned part-time worker." She moved around Nathan and reached for the knob. "Brody Mac? Is that you in there? Come on out, hon, this is Becca."

Shuffling sounded from inside. Slow, soft footsteps made their way to the door. The knob turned slowly and she moved back. Nathan caught her by the upper arms and she paused, waiting.

The door opened and Becca tensed. "Brody Mac?"

"Becca?" He had a deep but gentle voice.

Her muscles relaxed and she stepped into the doorway. She looked up. At six foot three, he had the build of a linebacker, the heart of a marshmallow and the mind of a ten-year-old. Brody Mac's head hung low and he peered at her through his lashes. "Hi, Becca."

"Brody Mac, what are you doing coming in here at midnight and scaring everyone?"

He stuffed his hands into the front pockets of his jeans and shuffled his feet. "I didn't have nowhere else to go."

"Anywhere," she corrected automatically.

"Yes, ma'am, that's what I meant."

"Come out here and sit down for a minute, will you? I need to get my pulse back under control."

Brody Mac stepped into the hall and spotted Nathan. He gasped and ducked back into the room, ready to shut the door. Becca followed him before he could. "Brody

Mac, this is my friend, Nathan. Get back out here and meet him, will you?"

"Is he going to shoot me? I saw his gun."

"No, of course he's not. I have my rifle, too, but no one is going to do any shooting, okay?" She noticed Nathan had the weapon out of sight and was walking toward the seating area in the large room.

Brody Mac exited the bedroom, his tentative footsteps snagging her heart. She held out a hand and he took it, his palm dwarfing hers. She led him to the sofa where he sat down and released her hand, keeping his gaze on Nathan. Jack bounded over to him and licked his wrist. Brody Mac laughed and scratched the dog's ears. "Hi, Jack."

Becca patted his arm, pulling his attention from the animal. "This is Nathan Williams. Say hi."

"Hi," Brody Mac said. He extended his arm but then pulled it back. Nathan held his hand out and waited. After a brief hesitation, Brody Mac gave a small smile and shook his hand.

"Nice to meet you, Brody Mac," Nathan said. "I didn't mean to scare you with the gun. I'm a cop."

Brody's almond-shaped eyes went wide. "A cop? For real?"

"For real."

"That's super cool. I like cops. They keep me safe."

"Yeah," Nathan said, his voice soft. "We sure do try to do that."

"Now," Becca said, "tell me what you're doing here."

"I had to leave home."

"Why?" she asked, but had a feeling she already knew the answer.

"This afternoon, Daddy came home and started yelling 'cause the tractor wouldn't start. Mama told me to go find someplace to stay. I was at the library for a long time then I walked here. I got lost a couple of times so I had to go home and find the way through the woods. That's why I got here so late."

Becca rubbed her eyes and glanced at Nathan. "There's a shortcut between his land and mine." To Brody Mac, she said, "Are your things still in the bedroom?"

"Yes, ma'am."

"Okay. You know you can stay here."

Nathan lifted a brow at her and she shrugged. "His daddy's not such a nice person, but Brody Mac here is a great guy."

Brody Mac shuffled and rubbed the palms of his hands up and down the sides of his legs. "But my daddy doesn't like me. He says I'm stupid." His lower lip quivered. "I'm not stupid, am I, Becca?"

Rage at the man's careless and needless shaming of Brody Mac burned in her heart, and her tongue wanted to blast the man. With effort, she controlled both and forced a smile. "Of course, you're not stupid. I know he's your daddy, but sometimes daddies are wrong," she said. "About a lot of things." She looked at Nathan. "Brody Mac's a hard worker and helps out around the ranch when school's not in session. He lives here in the bunkhouse during winter break and the summer." She bit her lip and studied her friend. "Looks like you might need to move in a little early?"

"Can I, Becca?"

"May I."

"Okay. May I? I'm almost done with school this year. I graduate in—" Brody Mac screwed his face up, then shrugged "—three weeks, I think. Just in time for Christmas."

"Something like that," Becca agreed.

"They have graduation in December?" Nathan asked.

Becca smiled. "This school does."

"I would have graduated in May, but they let me stay until Christmas. I'm twenty-one." He clapped his hands and grinned. "I'm all legal now."

"Congratulations," Nathan said.

"Thanks." Brody Mac grinned.

Becca stood. "All right, big guy, you've got three more weeks of school so that means getting up and getting there on time if you spend the night here. Can you do that?"

"I can. I can do it. I have my alarm clock by my bed. I can set it and everything. I'll show you."

"I believe you." She settled a hand on his massive shoulder. "All right, be sure to tell your mother what you're doing. She can choose whether or not to fill your father in. As for getting you to school, you can use the moped to get to the bus stop. You know where it is."

"Thank you, Becca."

"Sure, and just remember——"

"Roll the moped outta the barn so I don't scare the horses when I turn it on. I promise."

"Right. You'll do great."

He looked at Nathan. "I learned that last summer."

Becca couldn't help the slow curl of her lips. "The hard way."

Brody's eyes crinkled at the corners. "Yeah. The hard way." He rubbed his nose. "I don't think that horse likes me anymore."

"He likes you. Be sure to take the lock so you can chain up the moped."

"I will. Becca says some people have sticky fingers," he told Nathan. Then looked at his hands. "My fingers aren't sticky." He wrinkled his nose. "They only get sticky when I eat pancakes and ice cream."

Becca could see Nathan fighting a grin and something inside her shifted. He'd been her best friend growing up, the brother she'd never had and always wanted. Only right at that moment, she saw him in a different light.

And it wasn't as a brother.

She cleared her throat. "It's been a long day, guys. I'm heading to bed. Brody Mac, Nathan is staying here, too, so please don't use all of the hot water in the morning, understood?"

"Understood." He nodded then frowned. "You think my mama's going to be all right?"

"She always has been." Why the woman put up with her husband who took off for weeks on end then came home to drink and verbally abuse her and Brody Mac, Becca would never understand. But she could give Brody Mac a safe place to stay and make sure he had a full belly every day until his father decided to leave again. She ushered Brody Mac back to the bedroom. "Get some sleep, all right?"

"Thank you, Becca." The gentle giant hugged her, and Becca felt her throat grow tight as tears threatened. How anyone could be mean to this man-child was beyond her understanding. He shuffled into the room and shut the door.

"I'll get Clay to send someone out to his house tonight to check on his mother," Nathan said softly when she walked back into the den area.

"That'd be good," Becca agreed. "I can call her, too, and let her know where he is for tonight. Brody Mac's father isn't violent—not in the sense that he uses his fists on anyone. At least I don't think so. But he's sure got a mouth on him. Last time he was home, he came looking for Brody Mac and he and I got into it. He threatened to see me 'get mine' if I kept interfering in his family business."

Nathan stiffened. "What did he mean by that?"

"I have no idea and I didn't ask. I just wanted him off my property ASAP."

"I see. So why does he care where Brody Mac is if he just wants to belittle him?"

"I don't know for sure, but I suspect it's because Brody Mac is *his*. His to boss around, his to be mean to. He wants to control him and make him feel stupid while making himself feel powerful. It's how he gets his kicks."

"Sad."

"I know. And it's the same way with his wife. She's not exactly a mouse, but I think she's afraid of him— and he leaves her alone for extended periods of time so I think she just puts up with it when he's home and sighs in relief when he's gone."

Nathan shook his head. "I don't understand people like that. Even though I've worked with them and arrested a few, I just don't understand them." He paused. "Do you think that could have been him in the barn? The one who attacked you?"

She thought about it and shivered. "Maybe. But, like I said, as mouthy as he can be, I've never heard of him hitting or hurting anyone. I guess there could always be a first time, but I couldn't say for sure it was him in the barn."

"I'll get Clay to check into the man's whereabouts during the time of the attack. What's his name?"

"Jeff MacDougal." She gave a slow nod and picked up her rifle. "Checking his whereabouts during the attack might be a good idea." She frowned and looked at him.

"What is it?"

"I'm glad you're here, Nathan."

He blinked and his jaw tightened. "Why's that?"

"Mostly because it's good to see you, but I can't deny that having you here will let me rest easier." She walked to the door. "But I'll warn you. If Brody Mac's dad knows he's staying here—and he'll probably guess he is—he's likely to show up."

Nathan narrowed his eyes. "Then we'll be ready."

THREE

Early the next morning, Nathan stood in the door of the bunkhouse and watched Brody Mac leave on the moped. He liked the guy and was grateful that he hadn't used all the hot water just as he'd promised. He'd even cleaned up the sink and set out clean towels for Nathan. A roommate Nathan could appreciate. Unlike the guy he'd shared a dorm room with in his sophomore year at Vanderbilt. Nathan grimaced at the memory.

Turning slightly, he could see Becca out in the pasture filling up water troughs for the horses. She moved slow and a little stiff and he figured her back was bothering her. Nathan slipped on a pair of work gloves and headed out to help her.

As he walked down the dirt path that led to the pasture, a truck rumbled up the drive and pulled to a stop at the barn. Jack barked twice, then went to greet the newcomer.

Becca looked up, then set her bucket on the ground and pressed a hand to her back. "That's Zeb," she called. "Tell him I'll be there in a second, will you? I have two more troughs to fill."

"I'll do it for you."

She waved a hand. "I've got it."

"Becca—"

"I've got it. Thanks." She picked the bucket up and headed for the next trough.

"Stubborn woman," Nathan muttered as he headed toward the truck. A man in his early thirties climbed from the driver's seat. His stylishly-cut sandy brown hair dipped into his eyes.

Nathan nodded to the stranger. "Hi, there. I'm Nathan Williams."

Dark brown eyes met his and the man held out his right hand. "I'm Zeb Culbreth, Becca's vet. You're new around here, aren't you?"

"Just to the barn, but I was born and raised in Wrangler's Corner."

Zeb nodded. "I haven't lived here long myself. I moved here a few months ago when Aaron Starke hired me to work with his veterinarian practice. It's a friendly place and I've been making friends ever since, but I knew I hadn't met you before. Where've you been?" He smiled and Nathan couldn't help but like the guy.

"Nashville. I moved back here about a week ago," Nathan said.

"What was in Nashville?"

"Work, mostly. I decided I needed a break so came home while I try to figure out my next step. Becca hired me to help her out around here." It was true enough.

"Good for her. It's about time she hired some help. She's needed it ever since her accident and hasn't had enough of it. Her neighbors to the left are the Mac-Dougals and they have their issues."

"Yeah, I've met Brody Mac."

"He's a good kid."

"Actually, he's a man."

Zeb blinked. "Yeah, I guess so. Seems more like a

kid, though. Anyway, her neighbors to the right are the Staffords. Jean and Hank pitched in quite a bit right after her accident and still check in on her."

"The Staffords? Are they new to town? I thought the Howards lived there."

"The Howards moved a little over a year ago, and the Staffords moved in about six months ago. Nice people. Jean used to do some pro equestrian work. Was in shows and everything. So she and Becca hit it off famously."

Nathan shot a glance and a scowl toward the Mac-Dougal farm, then turned his attention back to the vet. "It's nice to know Becca's got at least one good neighbor."

"Yep. Of course, her cousins pitched in almost immediately after her accident—and they'd still be right over if she asked, but they've got their own businesses and whatnot and had to get back to them once Becca was on her feet again."

"And I feel sure Becca's not going to ask."

Zeb's eyes narrowed. "You know her well?"

"We were in high school together and were good friends before she moved to Nashville."

But this guy had only known her a few months and he sure had a lot of information on her. Had the man done his own research or had Becca shared it all with him?

A surge of jealousy flickered through Nathan and he shoved it away. He didn't have any right to feel jealous. She had moved on with her life and that was the way it was supposed to be. It was a small town and people talked. A lot. It wouldn't take Zeb long to get the scoop on Becca if he asked all the right questions. And besides, Nathan didn't have any interest in resurrecting feelings she didn't return.

Better to keep a protective barrier erected around his heart this time. Once she found out what he was up to, she'd hate him forever anyway. He did find it interesting that there'd been no mention of her parents helping or even visiting.

He couldn't help wondering where they'd been during such a hard time for her and what kind of severe falling-out would keep them from putting their anger aside to come to their daughter's aide. Surely her leaving the medical profession wasn't justification for cutting her out of their lives, was it?

He wanted an answer to that, but he wasn't going to ask Zeb. "What can I do for you?"

"I wanted to check on Pete, the horse that threw Becca."

"What caused him to do that, anyway? Becca's been on horses her entire life. I can't see her getting thrown—especially by a horse she knows very well."

"Even the most experienced riders can get thrown, but I know what you're saying. It does seem strange. Everyone still talks about her awards and everything. She's made the town proud. Well, until the drug rumors started."

"Yeah, I've heard the rumors." And he didn't want to discuss that either, but if he was here to investigate… "What do you think about those rumors? Any truth to them?"

"That Becca's involved?"

"Yeah."

The man scowled. "Absolutely not, so don't go saying she is or asking questions, understand? No need to get that all stirred up again. Not that it's exactly died down yet, but still…"

Nathan raised a brow at Zeb's quick defense and

lifted his hands in surrender. "I promise I won't stir that up." Interesting. The man's instant defense of Becca sparked his curiosity. But he'd think about that later. "So what about Pete?"

"From what I can tell, poor Pete had an abscess up under his hoof and was in major pain. When she tried to jump him, he balked."

Nathan nodded. "Makes sense. Just a freak accident, then."

Zeb shot him a funny look. "Yes, why? Is there some reason you think it *wasn't*?

Nathan shrugged. "Nope. Guess not."

"Hi, Zeb, glad to see you here," Becca said as she joined them.

"No problem. I heard you had some commotion out here yesterday. Are you okay?"

Her smile flipped. "I'm doing fine. People in town are talking, huh?"

"Of course. When anyone mentioned it to me, I told them to get the facts before they opened their mouths." He shrugged. "Some will, and sorry to say it, but some won't."

"I know. The fact is, I was attacked in my barn and Nathan here scared him off. Probably some junkie looking for something to sell."

"You need security out here," Zeb said. "It's not safe. Especially since your two helpers had to quit."

Becca frowned.

"What are you talking about?" Nathan asked.

She sighed. "I had two teenagers working for me, but…"

"But what?"

"But Clay came out to search my ranch for drugs because he found my cell phone number on a dead man's phone." Her jaw tightened and her eyes narrowed. "That's not exactly confidence inducing for the parents who were allowing their kids to work for me, so they made them quit."

Nathan winced. "Ouch."

"Yes." She shrugged and looked at Zeb. "I'm safe enough. Yesterday was a fluke. Nathan's living in the bunkhouse for now, and Brody Mac will soon be here for winter break. I'll be fine." She nodded toward the barn. "You know where the horses are. How long do you think you'll be?"

"A few hours. But I won't get in the way of anyone you've got coming in."

"Great."

Nathan handed her the cell phone he'd found on the table in the bunkhouse. "Are you looking for this?"

She rolled her eyes and took it. "Thanks. I'm always looking for that."

Zeb gave her a salute and headed off to do his job. Nathan looked at her. She had a streak of dirt across her forehead. "How's your back?"

"Hurting a little."

"I thought so."

She gazed out over the pasture. "It's not terrible, but I guess I'll take you up on your offer to finish up out there. Four horses are in the north pasture and I need them brought down. I need to conserve my strength for this afternoon, so I'm going to go sit and pay bills."

"What else is on the schedule today?"

"A special education class from the elementary school is coming out for a tour and some pony rides. There are six students and three teachers." She pressed a hand against the side of her head and looked around. "I should have put up some Christmas decorations to make the barn look more welcoming, but I just haven't felt up to digging them out." She sighed. "Oh well, I guess it doesn't matter. It won't affect the riding. After they leave, I have a physical therapy appointment then lessons this afternoon. One group lesson and two private."

"Head's hurting, too, huh?"

"I've had the occasional migraine since the fall."

Her grudging admission sparked his curiosity and he wondered why it was so hard for her to ask for help. "Is this one of those occasions?"

"Looks like it's going to be." She grimaced.

He gave her a gentle push in the direction of the house. "Go, forget the bills, take some medicine and lie down for a bit. I can handle things here."

"But—"

"I grew up on a horse ranch, just like you. I know what to do."

She sighed. "I know you do. Okay." She started toward the house, then turned back. "But promise you'll come get me if—"

"I promise. Go."

She went.

"I know you said you went to high school together, but do you have a history beyond that?" Zeb asked.

Nathan spun to find the vet behind him, wiping his hands on a cloth. "A history?" He shrugged. "No. Why?"

"Because I'm interested in her and wanted to make sure you weren't the competition."

Well, he'd thought he liked the guy, but Nathan had to bite his tongue on the first words that wanted to slip out. Instead, he drew in a deep breath and smiled even while he reminded himself that he wasn't interested in Becca. "No competition here," he said. "I'm just the hired help." Becca had a mind of her own. If she chose to date the vet, Nathan wouldn't get in her way.

Much. Maybe.

Zeb held up a hand. "You're sure? I mean, I'm only asking because I don't want to interfere. Just tell me the word and I'll keep everything strictly professional with her."

Okay, so maybe the guy wasn't so bad after all.

"There's nothing between us," Nathan said. "Nothing but friendship."

Liar, his heart whispered.

Becca wasn't sure how much time had passed from the moment she took the migraine pill to her roll over to look at the clock, but she thought it might have been about an hour and a half. She was just grateful the pounding had eased to a dull throb and the nausea had faded. Her back even felt much better. She eased her way from the bed and into the bathroom. One glance in the mirror made her grimace. She might feel better, but she looked like she'd been run over by a truck.

She washed her face, brushed her hair and her teeth and decided she wouldn't scare the children too terribly bad.

And what about Nathan?

Why did she care? She sighed. Because she did. Ever since he'd rescued her in the barn, her heart had started doing strange things around him. Things she didn't have time to investigate but found herself wishing she did.

A knock sounded on her front door. Becca slapped a hat on her head and made her way down the hall and into the foyer. She almost opened the door without looking but thought better of it. Glancing out the side window, she saw Nathan standing on her porch.

Tall, good-looking Nathan, with a dimple in his right cheek and shoulders just made for nestling against. She swallowed and wondered what was wrong with her. She'd never thought of Nathan in that way before. Why start now? Refusing to dwell on her crazy thoughts, she yanked the door open. "Hey."

"Are you feeling better? Your guests are here."

"I'm better, thanks."

"I've got Mason and Dixon saddled up and ready to go. You had them listed next to the kids' names on that clipboard in your office."

She wanted to hug him. "You're an answer to my prayers, Nathan Williams."

He flushed, endearing him to her even more. He ducked his head in exaggerated embarrassment. "Aw shucks, ma'am."

She swatted his arm and shut the door behind her. One glance at the sky spoke trouble. Clouds hung heavy and low. "It's going to storm."

"Yep."

"Well, let's do what we can do while we can do it. Once lightning starts, we'll have to close up."

Becca stepped out of her house and headed toward the group of kids. One of her greatest pleasures was helping the little ones ride. She gave the group of students and teachers a wide smile. "Welcome to Priceless Riding School. It looks like it's going to rain, but does anyone want to see if we can beat the storm and get some riding in?"

Five hands shot into the air. One young little girl, about eight years old, ducked behind one of the adults. Becca smiled. She hoped the child would watch her classmates having fun and decide to give it a try, but she wouldn't push her. "All right then, let's go out to the arena and do some riding." She glanced around and prayed whoever had attacked her the day before was long gone. She shivered at the memory but refused to let it ruin her day. With Zeb and Nathan nearby, everyone should be plenty safe.

Two hours later, the rain started with large drops, but the children had all ridden several times. All except the little girl. She'd watched and cheered for her friends but refused to get in the saddle herself. Maybe another day. Becca ruffled the girl's blond curls and led the group into the barn. Everyone laughed as they dashed for cover.

Nathan had the horses and Becca herded the children into the large room she'd set up for birthday parties and other fun activities. Today, they'd have snacks and drinks and restroom breaks. Crayons and pictures of horses were set out to be turned into masterpieces.

"Thanks for doing this, Becca." Sharon Hyatt, one of Becca's friends from high school, sidled up beside her. She also boarded a horse at the barn.

Becca smiled. "My pleasure."

"We almost cancelled, you know."

"What? Why?"

Sharon shrugged. "Because of what happened yesterday—and the rumors that the sheriff actually got a warrant to search your property for drugs."

"Right. Well, those aren't rumors, they're facts. He did search it."

"I told the powers that be if there was any danger, you would have called, and that if there were any drugs, the sheriff would have found them. But I didn't see any point in cancelling. They didn't like it much, but they like *me*, so…" She shrugged.

"Thank you for defending me. Yesterday was just a

fluke thing." She hoped. "Someone looking for something to sell—or the drugs I'm rumored to have on the property. I just happened to be in the barn at the time he came looking." She forced a smile to stiff lips. "There's no danger here." *Please God, let that be true.* "And there are no drugs, absolutely none." She *knew* that was true.

Why Donny had had her number in his phone, she didn't know, and likely never would. Just a strange coincidence. Or maybe he'd called her about boarding a horse and she'd called him back.

She talked to a number of people on a daily basis—new people calling to ask questions about finding a barn or lessons she taught. She didn't always remember their names. But it didn't explain the other two times he'd received a call from her number. Or the text. It was just strange. The fact that he'd been in trouble with the law on drug charges before bothered her, of course, but there was no way to connect everything. And that bothered her, too, because she was probably missing something. But what? If Clay couldn't figure it out with all of the resources at his disposal, what was she supposed to do?

"I'm going to come ride Lady Lou tomorrow afternoon," Sharon said. She looked up and frowned at the overhanging clouds. "I don't think today's going to work, but tomorrow should. It's been too long since I've given her a good workout."

"She's a gentle soul and was glad to see you today. Thanks for letting us use her for the kids."

"Of course."

Jack walked over and Becca scratched his ears, grateful that everything had gone well with no strange or dangerous incidents. It seemed since her accident, there had been a series of "mishaps." The mower's busted brake line, a missing feed bin she knew she'd just filled right before her accident, catching glimpses of strange lights in her barn but no one being there when she investigated. Just weird stuff. Nothing to be afraid of—except the attack earlier—but she had to admit, it was all starting to worry her. "I'm glad the kids were able to ride before the storm hit."

Sharon nodded and stole a glance at the sky through the barn door. "We'd better get going, though. It's just sprinkling right now, but the bottom is getting ready to fall out of those clouds."

Within minutes, the adults hurried the children through the light rain and herded them onto the small bus. All except one. "Wait a minute," Becca said, "where's the little blond girl? Jessica?"

Sharon frowned and did a quick head count. "She must still be in the barn. I'll get her."

Thunder boomed and they flinched as they ran back to the shelter of the barn. "Jessica?" Becca called.

No answer. Sharon added her voice to Becca's. Nathan stepped inside and shook his head. Water flew from his hair. "What's going on?"

"We're looking for Jessica." Becca felt a flicker of worry. "Check all the stalls."

Nathan frowned. "I'll look around outside. She liked watching the horses in the pasture."

"But it's raining," Sharon said, "she wouldn't go back out in this."

"Never know with a kid." He ducked back out into what had become a downpour.

Becca turned back to checking the stalls. A horse's agitated whinny brought her attention to the third stall from the end. She hurried to the door and looked in.

Jessica stood there, pale and trembling, her terrified eyes locked on something on the ground.

Becca followed the child's gaze and froze.

FOUR

Nathan stepped back into the barn, drawn back by Sharon's terrified call, to find Becca holding a hand out to the small girl. "Don't move, honey, don't move. Stay still like you're playing freeze tag."

"What is it?" he asked softly.

"A snake," Sharon whispered, and locked terror-filled eyes on his.

Nathan didn't hesitate. He grabbed the pitchfork from where it leaned against the wall and stepped to the stall. Thankfully, there wasn't a horse in it. Just the snake and the girl. Becca moved out of his way and he slipped inside.

The snake was about three feet long with a sub-rectangular pattern across its back. It slithered along the side of the stall straight toward Jessica but turned his attention to Nathan's entrance. Nathan brought the edge of the pitchfork down across the base of its head. The reptile protested but couldn't escape the pressure. "Get her out," Nathan said. "Then get me the ax."

Becca stepped forward and grabbed the little girl's hand. "Come on, honey, it's safe now."

Jessica scooted up close and Becca led her from the

stall. Sharon grabbed her in a hug and let her eyes lock on Becca's. "Thanks."

Becca nodded. "I'm sorry."

"Don't be. One has to expect snakes in a barn sometimes, right?"

Becca's lips tightened but she said nothing as she raced to the office to get the ax. She returned within seconds and passed it to Nathan. He took it and she motioned for the others to follow her out of the barn.

He waited until they were gone to take care of the snake. Once the unpleasant chore was done, he walked outside to stand next to Becca. They watched the little bus roll down the dirt road. As soon as it was out of sight, Becca's shoulders slumped.

"You okay?" he asked.

"No. Things keep happening and I just don't understand it."

"What kind of things?"

"Things! *Bad* things. The fall from my horse, the... the snake in the stall, the equipment that keeps breaking, fences that fall down. Everything!"

Nathan placed his hands on her shoulders and drew her to him, careful not to cause her pain—or make her uncomfortable if she wanted to pull away. She didn't. Her forehead fell against his chest and he stayed silent while she worked to get her emotions under control. She sniffed. "Sorry. I didn't mean to fall apart," she whispered.

"It's okay. You've had a rough time of it."

"Becca?"

Zeb. The vet. He'd forgotten he was still here. He'd come from the far pasture where he'd been working with the horses.

Becca moved from his arms and he felt a keen sense of regret that the semi-embrace had ended so quickly.

But she was already walking toward Zeb who had his bag in his left hand.

"I'm all finished," Zeb said. "All the horses have had their shots, Pete's abscess looks good and is healing nicely. I went ahead and filled the water buckets and cleaned out the last three stalls while you had the horses out."

"Oh, Zeb, thank you. You didn't have to do all that."

He shrugged. "I'm still building my client base. I didn't have any more calls this afternoon, so I had the time." He shot a smile at Nathan. "Aaron can't give me all of his patients."

"Guess not."

"Anyway, glad to help."

"You're great. Thank you." Becca patted him on the shoulder.

"Sure thing." A pause. "Something wrong? You look really stressed."

She told him.

"A snake? What kind?"

"I took a picture of it after I killed it. I've seen a lot of snakes around these parts, but never one like this." He held his phone out to Zeb. "Recognize it?"

The vet frowned. "No." He leaned closer. "Wait. I might. See the green tint to it?"

"Yeah."

"I think it's a Mojave green rattler."

Becca sucked in a ragged breath. "Whoa." She shuddered.

"Man." Zeb's eyes narrowed and he shook his head. "It's a good thing you didn't get bit." He rubbed his hands and looked around as though another snake might be waiting to strike. "Ah, anyway, I've got to go." His eyes drilled into Becca's. "Be careful, okay?"

"Yes. Thanks, I will."

He nodded, then raised a brow at Nathan before he climbed into his truck. Zeb headed in the same direction the school bus had gone only a few moments before.

Nathan blinked.

Zeb had obviously seen Becca in Nathan's arms and was jealous—and wondering at Nathan's claim that he wasn't competition. He should have just kept his mouth shut—or said something like they were figuring it out. Now the man would think he'd lied. Great.

Becca walked back to him. "You sure you need him?" he asked her.

"Who? Zeb?" She let out a low laugh. "Yes, pretty sure."

"But you're a doctor, you can take care of that stuff yourself, can't you?"

She frowned. "Maybe, but you know as well as I do that veterinarian medicine and human medicine are vastly different. I'd rather trust the animals to a vet."

"Yeah, I know, I'm just being silly." He shrugged. "So why not be a vet since it's obvious you love working with animals?"

She grimaced. "Believe it or not, I thought about it. And I can do some things a vet would do, but," she shrugged, "being a vet wasn't nearly as prestigious as being a surgeon."

He tilted his head, feeling sure there was more to the story. "And you wanted prestige?"

"No, not me. But I did want to please my father who had determined from my birth that his daughter would follow in his footsteps. So…there you have it."

"Ah."

"Yeah." She pressed a hand to her head.

He frowned. "Another migraine?"

She blinked and dropped her hand. "No, actually. I'm fine. Overwhelmed and stressed out, but fine."

He let out a low laugh. "You do realize you can't be overwhelmed and stressed out and be fine all at the same time, right?"

At first she didn't respond, but then she gave a tired chuckle. "I guess not. How about, I'm overwhelmed and stressed out, but I'm not in much pain at the moment. Which is nice."

"That works. And I'm glad. Are you hungry?"

"Starved."

"Got any food in the house? The bunkhouse needs to be stocked."

"Sure, and I can get that done tomorrow if you can manage until then."

"I can manage. Come on, it's getting close to lunchtime. I'll cook something."

"You cook?"

"I cook."

"Wow."

He definitely cooked. Becca finished off the last of the delicious chicken concoction and leaned back in her chair. Her back twinged, but at least there wasn't any sharp, shooting pain. "You get to stay," she said.

"What?"

Jack stretched out at her feet and she rubbed his belly with her toes. "You cook. Therefore, you get to stay. And Jack agrees because you feed him scraps as you work."

He laughed, speared the last hand-cut French fry, and popped it in his mouth. Becca studied him as he chewed. He'd aged a little since she'd last seen him. And had developed a few wrinkles around his eyes. But... he looked amazing.

"Are you okay?" he asked.

She sighed and dropped her fork onto the plate. "Okay how? I'm okay in the sense that I have my home, my business and I haven't had to declare bankruptcy yet, but..." She shrugged. "I don't know, Nathan."

"Tell me about the accident."

She gave a low laugh that held no humor. "I wish I could." At his lifted brow, she shook her head. "I don't remember a lot. Bits and pieces, but not much once the accident happened. And I think there are some things I don't remember that happened before. I get flashes, but nothing that I can string together to make sense of the day."

"So, tell me what you do remember."

She studied him then shrugged. "I might be an award-winning equestrian, but I still take lessons to keep my skills sharp since I'm not competing anymore. I don't remember this, but my trainer, Christine, was here. She said we saddled up and headed for the pasture. Christine said Pete seemed really antsy, but that she thought he was just restless and needed some exercise. Then once we got into the ring and I started him off for the first jump, he just went crazy and started bucking. I think I remember hearing Christine yelling, but it was all I could do to stay in the saddle. And then I just...couldn't. I remember falling and then waking up with paramedics surrounding me."

And something else. There was something else she needed to remember, but she just couldn't seem to grasp hold of the memory that continued to flicker at the edge of her mind. She tried to reach for it—and the pain in her temple hit her. She pressed a palm against the throbbing and cleared her mind.

"Becca?"

She opened her eyes to see Nathan hovering, his brows creased, worry staring at her. "I'm fine. It's just each time I try to think about that day, I get some sharp headaches."

"I understand."

"Do you mind if we change the subject?"

"Sure."

"Do you mind if I ask about your engagement?"

He froze for a split second, then nodded. "What do you want to know?"

"I heard you were engaged and broke it off."

"I was and did."

He didn't want to talk about it.

"Sorry, didn't mean to change the subject to one you don't want to talk about." Silence fell between them. Becca shifted and wished she'd kept her mouth shut. "Is it too soon?"

"No. It's okay. Not my favorite topic, but I can talk about it now. The hurt is in the past, it's just…"

"Just?"

He grimaced. "It's embarrassing now."

"Oh. Sorry. Embarrassing how?"

"Just how blind I was."

"Do you mind telling me about it?"

He drew in a deep breath. "I met Sylvia shortly after I moved to Nashville to take the job with the DEA. She was the sister of my partner. Pretty, an elementary school teacher…and a drug addict who had turned to dealing to support her habit."

Becca gasped. "Nathan. I'm so sorry."

"I am, too. One evening, just before the sun was

going down, we had a tip where drugs were being kept
and sold so we orchestrated a raid. Later, when it was
all over, we figured out that they knew we were coming but didn't know we'd moved the raid up a couple of
hours, so we still caught them by surprise. Sylvia was
one of the dealers I arrested. That's how I found out
what she was up to."

"That is…simply awful. Horrible."

"I was crushed. Betrayed. Furious. And embarrassed
for being so clueless. I don't think there's an emotion
you could name in that category that I didn't feel within
a twenty-four-hour period. And then I went numb, threw
myself into my work and swore off women."

"I don't blame you." She let out a laugh devoid of
humor. "And here you are, working for a woman who's
accused of being a possible drug dealer, runner, whatever. How can you stand to be around me?"

He looked at her, his eyes boring into hers. "If I
thought you were truly guilty, I wouldn't hesitate to turn
you in. But Clay found no evidence, you had no problem hiring me on the spot—a DEA agent at that—so…"

"So?"

"So, I don't think you're guilty."

"Even though a young man involved in drugs died
with my number in his phone?"

"Even though." He paused. "How did that happen
anyway? Do you know?"

"No, of course I don't. If I did, I would have told
Clay." She hesitated. "Are you sorry you decided to
come out and work for me?"

"No. That stuff doesn't match up with the girl I
knew in high school. Still doesn't." He smiled and then
shrugged. "I'll admit Sylvia messed up my judgment,
made me doubt myself, but you… I know you. And I've

watched you over the last couple of days. My judgment may be skewed, but I don't think it's nonexistent."

"Thanks for that."

He rubbed his hands together. "Let's not think about it anymore. I'm tired of heavy topics. What do you need me to do for the rest of the day?"

"You're going to use hard labor to keep from thinking?"

"Exactly."

She laughed, but there wasn't much humor in the sound. "All right, then, I need to clean out the rest of the stalls and look at the schedule for the lessons. The kids come after school."

"You have really full days, don't you? Kids riding in the morning and then again in the afternoon? That's a lot of work."

"Yes, but I love it." Thinking about the day, and the children who would arrive later, eased the headache. The time she spent with them was her happy time, her stress reliever. "You can help with the lessons, can't you? You haven't forgotten how to ride now that you're a big city cop, have you?"

He narrowed his eyes. "Wanna race?"

She laughed at the playful question. This time it was a real laugh and the sound actually surprised her. How long had it been? "No, not yet. Not with this back. But one day I might take you up on it."

They finished their food, and Becca cleaned the kitchen while Nathan went out to prepare for the lessons.

As she put the last dish into the cupboard, her cell phone rang. "Hello?"

"Ms. Price? This is Paul Gowen."

"Hi, Mr. Gowen, what can I do for you?"

"You can pack up those two horses of mine and have them ready to be transferred into the trailer. I have someone coming to get them in thirty minutes. I've got another stable I'm going to board them with."

Becca's breath left her in a whoosh. "Ah, okay, sure, I can do that, but do you mind me asking why?"

"You need to start paying attention to what people are saying about you in town. I don't know if it's true or not, but I can't take any chances or be affiliated with anything that has the rumor of drugs attached to it."

"Drugs? No! It's not true. They searched the whole place and didn't find anything. It was a lie."

"Sorry, little lady. Like I said, I can't take any chances. I'll give you two months' boarding fees for the inconvenience of pulling out on you so fast, but we're done." He hung up and Becca couldn't move. Her feet were frozen in place, her hand still pressing the phone to her ear.

Drugs. Why was this happening? *God, I don't understand. Please make this all go away.*

But he hadn't stopped her fall, and he hadn't made her parents understand her need for independence and the desire to own a stable and work with children. Why would she even bother to pray that he would help her with anything else? She felt guilty for the doubt, but figured God was big enough to deal with that, too.

Her phone rang. Grateful for the distraction, yet scared to death it was more bad news, she answered. "Priceless Riding School. How may I help you?"

"I did a little research, Clay, and that snake is not found in Tennessee. I think it was planted there during the party." Nathan pressed the phone to his ear and paced in front of the bunkhouse.

"But who could have done it—and why?"

"I don't know, other than to assume someone wanted to hurt Becca. Either by having a tragedy happen in the barn with one of the kids, or by killing her when she went to clean the stall. At this point, I'm just glad no one was hurt. But I'm telling you, something might be going on out here—as evidenced by the attack on her in the barn and now the snake's mysterious appearance— but Becca's not a part of it," Nathan said. "I think she's a victim in the whole thing."

"What thing?"

"Whatever *thing* you suspect there is." He paused to think, then asked, "Is there anyone who would benefit if Becca lost the ranch?"

"Well, her parents would be happy, but I don't know that they would benefit from it."

Nathan sighed and frowned. "Why are they so against her doing what she's doing? Just because she put her medical career on hold?"

"You'll have to ask her for the specifics, but I have a feeling it's not just because she walked away from a medical career, but because she might not go back."

"They should be proud of her for doing that. Most people get stuck in a job and only later regret they didn't chase their dreams."

Clay sighed. "Hey, I agree, but trust me, they're not happy about it."

"Would they go so far as to hire someone to scare her into giving up or cause her enough trouble that she went bankrupt?"

"Scare her? Maybe. My uncle is a tough man. He's hard to read and can come across really cold, so while I'm skeptical, I wouldn't rule it out. But, that snake could have killed her. I seriously doubt he'd go that far."

And just because the man had a chilly personality didn't mean he was a killer. Didn't mean he wasn't either, but...

"Anyone out for revenge?" Nathan asked.

"For what?"

"Interfering? Like MacDougal?"

"Brody Mac's father?"

"Yeah."

"He was the first one I thought of when I learned of the attack so I looked into him. He was in Nashville at a bar when Becca was attacked in the barn, so I'm going to say it's not him. Not that he couldn't have hired someone, but it wasn't him personally. And as for hiring someone..." He gave a short laugh. "I highly doubt that, too. He's flat broke as far as I know. His house is falling down around his wife's head and the city is getting ready to condemn it. Sabrina just learned their heat is out." Clay had married social worker Sabrina Miller and together they'd adopted two children and then had two of their own. Clay shook his head. "We have a guy at church who's going out there to fix it for Mrs. MacDougal as soon as he finishes up his paying job. Others have jumped in and offered to fix various things like the plumbing and the roof. So... MacDougal as Becca's attacker? No. Not unless..."

"Unless what?"

"Someone paid him to do it." Nathan heard Clay scribbling in the background.

"But he was in Nashville at the time."

"Maybe. What if that was a cover story whoever hired him came up with?"

"Is there any security footage you can get from the bar?"

"Working on that now. I'll let you know what I come

up with. Now, assuming MacDougal comes back clean, what else you got?"

Nathan rubbed his chin. "Who gets the ranch if something happens to Becca?"

"I don't know. That might be a good question to ask her."

"I'll do that."

From the corner of his eye, he saw Becca step out of the house, the screen door slamming behind her. She walked to the barn with a hand pressed against her lower back. The other hand swiped one cheek then the other and Nathan frowned. Was she crying? "I've got to go."

"Check back in if you learn anything more."

"Will do. You do the same."

Nathan hung up and slid the phone into his pocket. He hurried to catch up with Becca as she stepped into the barn. "Hey."

She stiffened, then sighed and turned. Yep, she was crying.

"What is it?"

"Nothing, not really."

"It's something. Now tell me."

She shook her head. "I had another client cancel a large-party trail ride, and one more person is pulling his horses from my stable."

"Because of the drug rumors?"

"Yes." She glanced at her watch. "I have to leave to go into town because I have a physical therapy appointment in about thirty minutes."

"I'll drive you."

"No, that's all right. I need you to stay here and keep an eye on Brody Mac. He texted me and said he would be here after he gets out of his last class."

"I wondered about that. He mentioned graduation coming up. He goes to college?"

She smiled. "No. It's a special school for people like Brody Mac. There's a bus that picks him up in the morning and brings him home in the afternoon. It's about a thirty-minute drive. He's learning a trade—all about agriculture and growing things—but it's on his level. He's doing really well and has stuck it out in spite of his father's discouragement." She glanced at her watch. "I've got to go."

"I'd rather you not go alone."

"I'll be all right. It's this place I'm worried about. I'm afraid if I leave it empty, someone will really come do some damage. And besides, Sharon's coming back to ride Lady Lou."

She had a point. "What about hiring a night security person or something?"

"That costs money. I don't have any to spare."

He suspected she barely had enough to keep the place going right now, but she wasn't ready to admit that fact to him. "Okay, then. You've got my number on speed dial. Use it if anything makes you nervous."

"I will, and the physical therapy office is just a couple of blocks down from the sheriff's office."

"Right, but you still have the drive there and back."

"I'll be careful." She reached out and hugged him. Nathan clasped her to him and simply held her, offering her whatever comfort his embrace had to offer. When she stepped back, he didn't want to let go, but he forced himself to release her. She patted his arm. "Thanks, Nathan."

Becca climbed into her truck and slammed the door. Nathan waved and watched her leave before dialing Clay's number again. When Clay answered, Nathan said, "Becca's heading to the physical therapist. I'm going to nose around a bit and see if I can find anything. You keep an eye out and make sure she gets there safely."

"Will do."

Nathan hung up and headed toward the house. With guilt weighing heavy on his heart, he stepped inside and stopped. "I don't want to do this," he said to the empty room. But someone was trying to hurt Becca, and the only way to help her might involve being sneaky and secretive.

He drew in a deep breath and walked down the hall to her office. Once there, Nathan took a reluctant seat in her chair and opened her laptop.

FIVE

Becca pulled into the parking lot of the physical therapy office and breathed a sigh of relief that she'd made the ten-minute drive into town with no incidents.

Maybe she was right. Maybe she was safe as long as she was off the ranch. The thought depressed her. Becca climbed out of her truck and walked toward the door of the office. It was getting late and her stomach was rumbling. She'd pick up something at the diner to take back for dinner.

"You stay out of my family's business, you hear me?"

Becca spun, wincing at the pull on her back muscles. Her heart thudded against her ribs when she spotted Jeff MacDougal leaning against the waist-high fence just outside the general store.

"I'm not in your family business. Brody Mac loves horses and ranch work. I simply let him help out." She paused. "And he's good at the work. He's a real help for me."

"Brody Mac don't have no business doing nothing for nobody. When he shows up, you tell him to get lost and get on home, you hear?"

"I hear. But I won't do it. He's a wonderful young man with a gentle heart. Why can't you see that? What do you have against him working and earning some money?"

He faltered for a moment. "He's really doing that good?"

"Yes. He really is."

Had she finally reached some soft spot in his anger-encrusted heart? For a moment, hope sprouted.

Then he scowled and straightened from his relaxed pose against the fence and pointed a finger at her. "Never mind that. If he wants to work, I'll be the one to put him to work, not some uppity debutante who don't know a mule from a donkey." He took a step toward her and she lifted her chin to stare him in the eyes. Backing down wasn't an option. And what right did he have to judge her? She probably knew her way around a ranch better than he did.

"As long as Brody Mac wants to help me out, he's got a place at my ranch. He's twenty-one years old and that makes him legal in the eyes of the law."

He laughed, spittle flying from around the wad of chew in his lower lip. "Lady, I don't care what the law says. Brody's my boy. I'm his law. And if I say you leave him be, you do so."

"Or what, Mr. MacDougal? You'll come on my property and attack me? Sneak around at night and try to scare me?"

He frowned. Then spat at her feet. "Now that ain't a bad idea." He turned on his heel and walked off.

"And I do so know the difference between a mule and a donkey!" She ignored the debutante dig. She *had* been a debutante, and while she didn't flaunt it, she wasn't ashamed of it, either. It was just a part of her growing-up years.

Becca's hands started to ache and she realized she'd

curled her fingers into hard fists. She blew out a breath and looked up to see Clay watching her. Tears arrived out of nowhere and she sniffed, refusing to let them fall. He walked toward her and she lifted her chin.

"I came in on the tail end of that. You okay?"

"Just fine."

"Do I need to go after him?"

"Only if you can arrest him for being a jerk and a lousy father."

He grimaced.

"That's what I thought." But he could raid her home and search for drugs she didn't have.

"Becca—"

"I'm fine, Clay. Don't let me keep you." She opened the door and stepped inside.

"Sabrina misses you."

She sighed and lowered her chin to her chest for a moment. "I miss her, too—and your kids," she said without looking back. Then she let the door shut behind her, but she didn't move. Immediate guilt slammed her. She didn't have to be rude to him.

Becca opened the door to apologize, but he was already walking back toward his office. He was within shouting distance, but she was going to be late if she didn't get back inside. With a frustrated sigh, she ran a hand over her messy ponytail.

Well, she could call him then. That wouldn't take too long. It wasn't right to be mean to the man when he was only doing his job. She snagged her phone from her back pocket, proud of herself for remembering to bring it. At the moment she began to dial, Bart Gold stopped him and began to talk. Becca grimaced. That conversation would go on for a while. And even though

Clay might appreciate the interruption, she decided the apology would have to wait.

Becca stepped back inside and looked around the large open room, taking in the busy, yet laid-back, atmosphere. She knew the exercises to do, and knew she could do them at home. She just couldn't give herself the massage she needed to loosen up the muscles. And truly, she really didn't mind coming into the office.

The trip into town was just as therapeutic for her mind as it was her body. It was the only time during her week that her muscles actually relaxed.

Christmas music filtered through the ceiling speakers, softly, barely there, but loud enough to enjoy.

Christmas.

She hadn't forgotten it was coming, but she sure hadn't done a thing at the barn to get ready for it. Making a mental note to ask Nathan to pull the Christmas decorations out of the attic tomorrow morning, Becca moved into the therapist's sight line.

Julie, the thirty-something woman, smiled and waved her over. "Hi, Becca. Are you ready to get started?"

"Sure."

But while she went through the motions of her appointment, MacDougal's threatening words and laser-like glare returned to the forefront of her mind. Was he the one causing all of her problems? And if so, how did she go about proving it? And was the fact that she allowed Brody Mac to help her out on the ranch really that much of an issue with him?

Apparently.

So what was the right thing to do? Forbid Brody Mac from coming to the ranch?

She shuddered at the idea. No, she couldn't hurt him like that. Then again, MacDougal was his father, and

Becca wondered if she should respect that in spite of the fact that MacDougal did nothing to inspire that emotion in her—or anyone else he came into contact with.

God? What do I do?

Nathan sat back with a thump. For the past thirty minutes he'd scanned Becca's laptop—her, much to his disgruntled surprise, nonpassword-protected laptop—and came up with nothing but financial records that showed she was barely making it with a full stable.

If clients kept cancelling and pulling their horses, she'd soon be forced to sell. Or fall into foreclosure. Her private emails were few and far between, only the occasional communication with her cousins, Sabrina, Amber and Zoe. Usually initiated by the Starke women checking on her by asking if she needed anything. Her answer was always the same. "I'm fine, thanks for checking."

He'd have to talk to her about that. Now he needed to know if she had a landline. With all the trouble she was having, installing an alarm system might be the best way to go. Certain ones would be too expensive for her, but sometimes companies ran specials for complete installation and all equipment with no money down. But he wasn't sure she'd want another monthly payment. Nathan saw a fax machine, but it wasn't hooked up.

"What are you doing in here, Mr. Williams?"

Nathan jerked and looked up to see Brody Mac in the doorway. He'd been so engrossed in his snooping, he'd failed to hear the man come in. Nathan frowned. How had he missed those heavy footsteps? He shook his head. He'd been away from the action for too long. "Hi, Brody Mac. I didn't hear you come in."

Brody Mac shifted from one foot to the other, his

hands clasped in front of him. "This is Becca's office. You shouldn't be in here."

Nathan stood. "It's okay. I'm just trying to help her out."

The young man shifted again then shrugged. "Okay. As long as you're helping her. Becca's a good woman. She's nice to me."

"I agree. She's a very good woman. I like her a lot."

Brody Mac grinned. "Okay, then." He stepped into the room. "Can I..." He paused and cleared his throat. "I mean, *may* I help you help Becca?"

"Sure, you can help. Do you know if Becca has a landline?"

"A what?"

"A phone that works when it's plugged into the wall. Not a cell phone, but..." How else could he put it?

"Oh, you mean like a cordless phone? Mr. Jacobs has one in his classroom to call for help if he needs it."

"Yes, like that." Cordless. Duh.

"No, she doesn't have one. She only has her cell phone. She said the cordless phone was too expensive."

"Okay. That was a big help. Thanks, Brody Mac." He clapped his hands together and rubbed them. "One other question."

"Sure."

"Do you know where Becca keeps her Christmas decorations?"

"They're in the attic. I helped her a lot last year, but when I asked her about it this year, she said she would get to it later." He shrugged. "I guess it's not later enough yet."

"Will you show me?"

"I sure can." Brody Mac led him down the hall and stopped at the end of it. "Up there."

"You want to do a little decorating?"

The man grinned, childish delight in his kind eyes. "Sure."

For the next thirty minutes, he and Brody Mac unloaded the decorations and started putting them out. Fortunately, Brody Mac was familiar with how Becca decorated and was able to quickly place things where they went.

In the attic, Nathan found an artificial tree with the lights still on it. He got it down and set it in front of the bay window in the living area. Becca would see it when she drove up.

He glanced at his watch. Time to get moving. "Hey, Brody Mac, you about done?"

"Yes." He hung the last ornament on the tree and plugged in the extension cord. The tree burst into multicolored twinkles and Brody Mac clapped his hands. "It's awesome."

Nathan agreed. "Think Becca will like it?"

"I think she'll love it."

He patted the young man on his arm. "Thanks for your help, I appreciate it. You're a good guy, Brody Mac."

Brody Mac enveloped Nathan in a bear hug and lifted him off his feet. Nathan laughed when he was finally on the wood floor again and gave the man a gentle push toward the door. "I think we're all done in here. Why don't we go outside and see what needs to be done for the lessons? The riders are going to be here soon."

"Okeydoke."

Brody Mac headed out the door and Nathan let out a low breath. He'd have to be a bit more careful in his searches. But the good thing was he hadn't found anything that said Becca was involved in drugs. Of course, he'd just had time to go through her financials on her laptop. He'd have to find another time to search her files and desk.

And at least he'd gotten part of her house decorated for her. He hoped it would be a good surprise and she wouldn't be disappointed that she hadn't had a hand in it. Guess he'd find out when she got back.

Until then, he'd do what he could to make sure she had to do as little as possible upon her return. He stepped outside and shivered. The temperature was dropping and he was grateful for his heavy coat and gloves.

Nathan found Brody Mac in the barn. The man looked up when he stepped inside. "I'm just getting the horses ready for the lesson." He pointed to a sheet of paper hanging on the wall. "See that list? That's how I know what horses she's using. She put that up there for me, you know."

"That's great. Want some help?"

"Sure thing, Mr. Williams."

"Why don't you just call me Nathan?"

"Okay. And you can call me Brody Mac."

Nathan laughed. He liked Brody Mac and admired Becca for taking him under her wing. And he saw why Becca was so fierce in her defense of the guy. Not only was he a gentle soul, he worked hard. Even better, he also knew his way around a barn and horses as well as Nathan did.

They worked together and Nathan sobered as he considered his deception. Becca would be back soon, and he thought seriously about telling her everything, but would she let him stay if she knew how he came to be there? And if she told him to go while the person who wanted to harm her was still out there, there wouldn't be any way he could keep her safe.

He placed the last saddle on the back of a gentle mare, and by the time he had the cinch tightened and the stirrups raised for shorter legs, he'd made up his mind.

He'd keep his mouth shut for now and pray that when the time came for him to lay it all out there for Becca, she'd find it in her heart to forgive him.

Becca finished her therapy and sat on the bench for the next five minutes while she did her best to find the energy to move. The twenty-minute massage that went along with the strengthening exercises had nearly put her to sleep. She felt more wiped out now than when she put in a full morning's work at the barn. But her back felt much better.

Finally, she gathered her things, slipped on her jacket and headed for her truck.

"Becca?"

She sighed and turned. "What now, Clay?"

Having him lurking, waiting on her to come out of the physical therapist's office, sent all thoughts of apologizing out the window.

"Are you ever going to forgive me?"

Becca turned. "Probably. One day." *Apologize.* She swallowed. "But I'm sorry I was rude to you earlier." There.

"Thanks. I get that you're mad at me. And, the truth is, I don't really believe you're involved in anything like drugs, but I have to follow where the evidence takes me—and unfortunately it took me to your ranch. I hope you understand that."

She did, but it didn't make it any easier to swallow. "Clay, I don't know why there would be a record of calls on Donny's phone from me. It doesn't make any more sense to me now than it did when you questioned me about it." She paused. "But it's probably because I'm always leaving my phone lying around somewhere." Not so much since the attack, though. "Sometimes I leave it in the barn in spite of the fact that I should have it on me at all times when I'm out riding." But when she was giving lessons, she didn't want to be distracted and so had gotten in the habit of just leaving the device in the barn while teaching. "Anyone could walk in and use it."

"But why? Most people have their own cell phones. They don't need to use someone else's." He lifted his hat from his hand to rake fingers through his already-mussed hair. He replaced his hat. "And besides, do you know how unlikely that whole idea is? One call, yeah, maybe. I'd be willing to buy that. But three?"

Becca's frown deepened. It did sound bad when he put it like that. She sighed. "Again, I don't know. All I know is I'm losing business because of your investigation and I don't know how to prove I'm not—"

Her voice cracked and she snapped her lips shut.

"Aw, Becca. I'm sorry. I really am."

Tears gathered and she swiped them away. It seemed all she did lately was cry. "I am too, Clay."

He sighed and walked over to hug her and she let him. Maybe forgiving him wasn't so far off.

"Have you talked to your parents lately?" he asked.

"No."

"Why not?"

"Because even if I bothered to call, they wouldn't pick up. And if I left a message, they'd just erase it. Do you know how much that hurts?"

"Wow. It's that bad?"

She stepped back from him and lasered him with

all of the frustration and anger that had built since her fall. "It's that bad."

He winced. "I'm sorry. Really."

She wilted, all the fight draining from her. "Yeah. So am I." Becca climbed in the truck. "I've got to go. I've got lessons to give this afternoon." At least she hoped she did. Truly, she was worried no one would show up.

"Come to Mom and Dad's for dinner on Sunday. Bring Nathan."

"We'll see. I'll talk to you later."

Becca decided she was too sapped to stop at the diner and knew she had peanut butter and jelly and chips at home. It wouldn't be the best meal she'd ever fixed, but it would do for tonight.

She dropped her cell phone into the cupholder for easy reach should she need it and then backed out of the parking spot and turned the truck toward home. Life was simply not fair these days, but she knew fair wasn't guaranteed. She was just going to have to take each day one hour at a time and pray things turned around for the better. *Please God, let things get better.* Some days she wasn't sure her prayers even reached heaven, but taking God at his word was one thing she was working on, and He'd promised to "never leave her nor forsake her." So she kept praying.

Becca braked to turn onto the main road that would lead her out of town and to the ranch. She made the turn and looked into the rearview mirror. An older-model sedan followed her. She tensed. Her next glance caught the car turning off onto one of the side roads. Becca let out the breath she'd been holding.

"Okay, don't start getting paranoid."

But was it paranoia when someone had attacked

her in the barn? Was it paranoia that things kept going wrong on the ranch?

Maybe. But she'd rather be paranoid and overly sensitive than oblivious and dead.

The drive up the mountain went smooth until she noticed another vehicle behind her. Again, her muscles tightened and her fingers flexed on the wheel. The white truck drew closer. Becca pressed the gas pedal but then let off. She'd let the truck go around her if he was in that much of a hurry. She slowed. He closed in fast. Too late, she realized he wasn't going to pass. Instead, he rammed the back of her truck.

Becca cried out and spun the wheel to keep the vehicle on the road. Another slam sent her into a spin. She screamed and stomped on the brakes. Her truck slowed, but the pedal felt squishy and then went to the floor.

In horror, she realized she was headed straight for the side of the mountain. Becca spun the wheel one more time and managed to keep from going over but it put her face-to-face with the person trying to kill her.

He gunned the engine of his vehicle and Becca slammed hers into reverse then hit the gas. She lurched backward and the attacker flew past her.

Becca hit the brakes and this time the pedal didn't even pause as it slammed against the floor once again.

She continued to move backward and dropped over the edge of the mountain road.

SIX

As Nathan led the last horse out of the stall and tied it to the railing, his phone rang. He glanced at the screen and noted Clay's name. "Yeah?"

"I'm going looking for Becca. I think her brake line is leaking," Clay said.

Nathan stilled. "What?"

"I would have called sooner, but I got stopped by the mother of a kid I arrested last week. Anyway, when I was done with her, I noticed a puddle of fluid left behind by Becca's truck. Pretty sure it's brake fluid. I called you because she's not answering. I don't think it's possible, but is she there yet?"

"No. Not unless she managed to sneak in without me hearing her." Which she could have done if he'd been in the barn. But he was pretty sure Jack would have alerted him. "Hold on a second, let me check." He looked out of the window of the bunkhouse. "I don't see her truck."

"Check the house."

Nathan walked over to the house and stepped inside, the screen door slamming behind him. "Becca?"

No answer. He checked the rest of the house. "She's not here, Clay."

"I don't like this," Clay said.

"I don't, either."

"Jeff MacDougal looked to be harassing her a bit in town. I tried to get her to tell me what was going on, but she wasn't interested in talking to me."

"I'm on my way." Nathan raced back to the bunkhouse to grab his keys and his gun and head for his truck. "Brody Mac! Brody Mac!" Back to Clay, he asked, "Did he follow her?"

"Didn't notice him doing so and I watched for a bit."

The young man came running from the barn. "What is it, Nathan? Is something wrong?"

"I'm not sure. Can you handle the trail ride?"

Brody Mac's eyes went wide. "You mean all by myself?"

"Yes."

"Um. I think so. I know all the kids coming and they like me. Their teacher does, too." He gave a shy smile.

"Okay, you're on your own. You have my number if something comes up."

"Okay." Brody Mac straightened his shoulders and thrust his chest out. "I'll do a good job. I promise."

"I know you will."

"But maybe Ms. Jean could come help me. Just in case?"

Nathan liked that idea. He would worry to death about leaving Brody Mac in charge, but he was more worried about Becca and her driving the winding road to the ranch with no brakes. And no way to call for help.

"I've got to see if someone can come out here to help with the lessons. Brody Mac suggested Jean."

"I'll send someone out there," Clay said. "Brody Mac knows his way around there pretty well, but he's right. It wouldn't hurt to have someone else there. From a liability standpoint. You get on the road and I'll see if Jean can help."

"That would be great. It's too late to cancel." And if he did, it would hurt Becca's business even more. "I'm sure her clients will be here any second." He'd probably pass them on his way to search for Becca, but he wouldn't have time to stop and explain.

Nathan threw himself behind the wheel of his truck and within seconds was careening down the long drive. He'd make his way toward town and keep his eyes open for Becca and pray Clay was wrong about the fluid belonging to her truck.

"I'm heading that way. We'll come at her from both directions so hopefully one of us will spot her pretty quickly."

Nathan made the turn that would put him on the road Becca should be on. He turned the heat up and let his eyes scan the area in front of him. Side to side, looking for Becca's vehicle.

A muffled crack reached him and he hit the brakes. The truck slowed and Nathan lowered his window. The same sound followed the first one. This time Nathan heard it loud and clear. "Did you hear that?"

"Yeah. That was a gunshot."

Becca screamed as the second bullet shattered her front windshield. She'd been fortunate in that when she went off the edge of the road, she hadn't been going that fast and had simply rolled backward into a tree. At least she'd thought she'd been fortunate until someone started shooting at her.

She sat frozen in the driver's seat, unsure whether to get out or stay in the fragile protection of the vehicle. Although, if he was shooting at her, he knew where she was. She'd already unhooked her seat belt and pushed the airbag to the side. Staying low, she opened the door and rolled out of the seat. Landing hard on the cold ground, Becca groaned at the pull on her back.

Then forgot about the pain as another shot took out her driver's-side window. The truck shifted, but she rolled under it anyway.

Fear hammered her heartbeat against her chest and she reached into her coat pocket for her phone. Only to remember she'd left it in the cupholder. No telling where it was now. Fighting the panic that wanted to consume her, she lowered her pounding head to the ground and tried to get her breathing under control. What was she going to do? How was she going to get out of this one without getting shot? She wasn't worried about the truck running over her. It was high enough off the ground that even if it went over the edge, it would pass right over her.

But the guy shooting…what if he came looking for her?

She had to find her phone.

No, she had to run. She couldn't stay here. Woods surrounded her, containing steep drop-offs and some hills and valleys. When darkness fell, she didn't dare try to find her way as she'd likely walk right off a cliff.

She pictured the landscape above her. If she walked parallel to the road, it was possible she could climb up farther down than where her shooter would look for her.

Or maybe she'd just make herself an easier target.

God, please. What do I do?

Becca lay still and listened. No more gunshots, no footsteps, but no sound of a vehicle leaving, either. At least she didn't think so. Her pulse thundered in her ears.

Was he just standing up there, watching? Did she

dare crawl out from under the truck to assess the situation? She had no choice.

She wiggled to the edge and prayed the truck continued to hold while she was now in the path of the tires. She peered out from under the belly of the vehicle and scanned the edge of the road where she'd gone over.

Nothing.

But she hadn't heard him leave. Now what?

Another shot sounded and the tire next to her head erupted with a whoosh of air.

She rolled back under the truck and squeezed her eyes shut while she thought of what to do next.

"Police! Freeze!"

Becca's eyes popped open. "Clay!"

"Becca?"

That was Nathan. "Down here!"

Oh thank you, Jesus. Thank you.

She slid out from under the truck once more, careful of her back, and looked up to see Nathan looking over the edge of the short cliff she'd rolled down.

"I'm coming to get you. Just hold on." He glanced back over his shoulder. "Clay! I need rappelling gear or a rope or something."

Clay appeared beside Nathan. "Becca, you okay?"

"Yes. Don't let him get away!"

"I've already called in the vehicle description. Unfortunately, I didn't get a look at the guy as he was getting in his truck as I drove up. I couldn't go after him until I made sure you were okay."

"Fine. Just get me up, will you?"

"Absolutely. Hold on."

Becca waited, shivering in the chilly temperatures. A stiff wind blew across her, and she tugged her coat tighter around her throat then shoved her hands into the pockets. She'd taken her gloves off during the drive.

In less than a minute, Nathan flung a rope over the side and it landed near her. "I'm coming down."

"No. I can climb up. Just stay there."

"You sure?"

"I'm sure." She grabbed hold of the rope and tied it around her waist in a triple knot. "Okay, pull me up."

With freezing hands, she held tight and walked up the steep hill, placing one foot in front of the other while Nathan helped her by keeping the rope taut and pulling it up with her.

Her back sent warning signals, but at least it didn't keep her from climbing. She could see the lights from other law enforcement vehicles and hoped those going after the person who'd shot at her were able to catch him. She *really* needed them to catch him.

Finally, she reached the top and Nathan assisted her to the edge of the road where her legs gave out. He caught her and lowered her to the asphalt.

And the tears came. Again.

Nathan sat down beside her and wrapped his arms around her. "It's okay," he whispered against her hair. "It's okay."

"No." She sniffed and used the sleeves of her coat to scrub the tears from her cheeks. "It's not okay. Since everything had happened at the ranch, I thought I would be safe enough away from it. But I guess I'm not."

"And I'm kicking myself for letting you go alone."

"I didn't really give you a choice."

"I had a choice, but—" He shook his head. "No sense in rehashing a bad decision. Let's just learn from it. Did you see who did this?"

"No. But I had words with Jeff MacDougal right

before my appointment. Clay was there. He saw most of it, I think."

"He did. And he was watching for you when you left. Clay's the one who spotted your fluid leak."

Clay approached. "I've got a guy who's tracking MacDougal down now. We'll pull him in for questioning."

"Did he look like MacDougal?" Clay asked.

"I couldn't tell as I only saw his back. His build could have been similar, but he was hunched over and moving fast to get in his truck."

"Hair color?" Nathan asked.

"I don't know. He had on a hat."

"So, what you're saying is you've pretty much got nothing," Nathan said.

"Pretty much, sorry."

He gestured toward the cliff. "Your truck is done for and will need some work before it'll be ready to run again. I've got a tow truck on the way. Once we get it up here, you can get what you need from it and Nathan can see you get home safely." He pinched the bridge of his nose. "I'm shorthanded right now, Becca. I'd put someone full time on your ranch, but I simply don't have the manpower. What would you think about moving in with my parents?"

She shuddered. Not at the thought of living with his parents, but at the thought of leaving her ranch vulnerable and open to whoever wanted to come in and do whatever they wanted. Like run drugs. She drew in a deep breath. "I'm not above admitting I need help. But I can't leave the ranch. The animals need to be cared for. I have clients depending on me—the ones I have left, anyway. I mean, even if I agreed to leave, I'd still have to have coverage of the place, have someone come in and take care of it. And, not only do I not have the funds to cover that kind of help, who knows if that would put someone else in danger?" She shook her head. "Leaving's not really an option."

"What about your neighbors?" Nathan asked. "The Staffords?"

"No. They're sweet, but a bit older. They were able to help out a bit when I had the fall, but it was really Clay, Aaron and Zoe and the others who kept the place going for me. I don't feel right asking them for more help when they have their own places to keep up with."

Clay nodded. "We wouldn't mind, you know that."

"I know, but…no."

"But…yes. I'm going to ask Aaron and the others if they can swing by at least once during the day to check on you. And you have Brody Mac and Nathan there. That will help, too." He held up his phone. "I've got to call Sabrina first and let her know what's going on and that I'm going to be delayed in getting home."

He turned away to get started on his calls and shivers wracked her. The temperature was going down and would hit in the midthirties by the time the sun disappeared on the horizon. Nathan must have noticed her tremors. "All right. Let's get you in the truck and warmed up."

Becca stood and winced at the jolt of pain in her back. But it wasn't horrible. She had hope that maybe all of the physical therapist's hard work hadn't just gone down the drain.

She let Nathan lead her to his truck and help her into the passenger seat. He leaned over her to crank up the heat before walking around to the driver's side to climb in. He fastened his seat belt. "Are you sure you don't need to go to the hospital?"

"I'm sure."

"Your back is hurting. You might need an X-ray to make sure you haven't hurt it worse."

"It's not hurt any worse. If it was, I would know—and I'd get someone to look at it. Trust me, it's not as bad as I was afraid it might be."

"All right, then. You're a big girl. I guess it's your call."

"Thanks."

The wrecker arrived and Becca placed a hand on Nathan's arm. "Wait, please? I'd like to get my purse from the truck if you don't mind."

"Of course not."

Twenty minutes later, she had her purse tucked on the floorboard at her feet.

Nathan climbed back into the driver's seat. "Ready?"

"More than."

He did a three-point turn and headed back toward the ranch, leaving the ugly scene behind.

Becca stared out the window and Nathan wondered what she was thinking about. The attack? The wreck? What she was going to do for a vehicle?

Probably all of the above.

She turned toward him about a mile from the ranch. "I guess I've lost all my clients after this afternoon."

"I don't know. I know you don't want to ask her for any more help, but Jean came and took over for you."

Tears spilled over and onto her cheeks. She closed her eyes and Nathan almost pulled the truck over so he could hold her once more. She drew in a ragged breath. "Sorry I'm such a weeping willow lately. I haven't cried like this in a while."

"No need to apologize. You've got some good reasons for tears."

"Maybe. I'll have to do something special for Jean. Thanks for calling her."

He started the truck up again. "I didn't. It was Clay's idea. Well, actually, it was Brody Mac's idea. Clay just made the call."

"She loves Brody Mac. Between the two of them, maybe things are okay after all."

Nathan turned onto her property and then pulled to a stop at the top of the horseshoe-shaped drive. He climbed out of his seat and walked around to help her out.

Jack ran out of the barn to greet her, dancing at her feet. She scratched his ears and he trotted off, happy with his little dose of attention.

Once she had her feet firmly on the ground, Nathan let his hands linger on her arms to make sure. "Want me to help you into the house?"

"I'm not an invalid."

"I know."

She sighed. "And I'm sorry. I shouldn't snap at you. Not after all you've done for me today. Thanks for the timely rescue."

"Anytime." He paused. "Although, I have to say, let's not have it happen again anytime soon."

She smiled. "That works for me. I just want to check on the horses and then I'll go inside and lie down."

"I'll take care of the horses. You go. Take a pain pill, too, and sleep."

She hesitated. "The pain isn't that bad."

"But you'll sleep better. And if we're going to fight whoever is doing this to you, you're going to need all the strength you can get."

Still she didn't agree. He tilted her chin to look her in the eye. "What?"

"What if something happens? If I take a pain pill, I won't wake up—at least not in a condition to fight back. I'll be groggy and—"

"I've already taken care of it. Temporarily, anyway."

"What do you mean?"

"I have friends in Nashville who can come help me out for a couple of days. If we cover this place up with security, it can give you some healing time—and Clay some time to go through any evidence he might gather from your wreck."

She bit her lip. Then nodded. "Okay. If your friends don't mind coming to help, that would be great." She shifted out of his reach and he wanted to pull her back. "But I can't pay them much."

"We'll work out the details. They're friends, they won't need much."

She walked stiffly toward the barn.

"Hey, I thought you were going inside."

"I just want to check on the horses."

He planted his hands on his hips and scowled at her. "You are one of the most stubborn people on the face of the planet."

"I know."

She sounded completely serious. Like it was a flaw she'd long ago accepted. She kept walking, stopping only to wave at Sharon who was putting Lady Lou through her paces in the ring. Sharon waved back and rode over. "Are you okay? You look pretty rough."

"I had a car wreck. Or a truck wreck, I suppose is a better way of putting it."

Sharon gasped. "What happened?"

"Just a reckless driver not caring that other people were on the road with him."

Nathan glanced at her, noting the lack of details in her simple answer.

"Other than a few bumps and bruises, I'm fine," Becca said.

"Man, I'm sorry."

"I am, too, but I'm alive and that's all that matters."

"What about the other person?"

"He's fine, too." Unfortunately.

"I'm glad you're okay." Lady Lou tossed her head and Sharon laughed. "This girl is impatient to get back at it."

"Go ahead. I'm just going to check on Pete."

Sharon rode off and Becca headed back toward the barn. She stepped inside and Nathan followed. When he shut the door behind him, he saw her standing at Pete's stall, stroking the horse's nose. "He hasn't been right since he threw me."

"What do you mean?"

She shrugged. "I don't know. Just more skittish, I guess." She looked around. "Where do you think Brody Mac is?"

"The bunkhouse?"

"Maybe." Frowning, she stepped into the feed room. "There's feed all over the floor. I guess he fed the horses. It's weird, though, he doesn't usually leave a mess like this." She paused and looked at him. "Was I wrong in not telling Sharon the whole truth about the wreck?"

"You mean, are you putting her in danger by leaving out the fact that the wreck was caused by someone trying to kill you?"

"Exactly."

"I don't know, to be honest."

She sighed. "I think I should tell her that someone is out to get me, and that if she comes around, she could get hurt, too. In fact, I think I should tell all my clients that."

"What will that do for your business?"

"Well, it won't help, that's for sure. It will probably do more damage than the rumors of drugs on the property." Her phone rang and she snagged it. "Hello?"

Nathan didn't mean to eavesdrop, but she didn't bother to try to have any privacy. "Thanks so much, Jean, I appreciate your help. Uh-huh. What?" She paled and met his eyes. "They did?"

Nathan moved fast and helped her into a chair next to Pete's stall. She sat with a thud and dropped her forehead into her free hand while she pressed the phone against her ear with the other. "What did you say?"

Nathan wished she'd put it on speaker so he could be privy to the discussion, but figured she'd tell him soon enough.

"Okay, thanks again, Jean. I can't tell you how much I appreciate you. I'll talk to you later."

She hung up and Nathan saw her fighting tears. Her despair was almost a physical thing, grabbing his heart and making him want to promise to fix everything if only she would smile at him.

If only he could. He dropped to his knees in front of her and took her hands. "What did she say?"

"Well, the lessons showed up today and everything went well according to Jean, but apparently as they were leaving, one of the leaders said they won't be coming back due to my sketchy reputation. Jean said they weren't happy that I wasn't here and are demanding a refund."

"They got their lesson, you don't owe them anything."

"I know. And I'll tell them that." She blinked rapidly and shook her head. "What am I going to do, Nathan? I'm going to lose this place if something doesn't happen to turn this around."

"What about asking your parents for help?"

Her head snapped up. Weariness vanished and the fire returned to her eyes. "Never. So don't bring that up again, okay?"

He blinked. "Okay." He paused. "Are they really that awful?" He truly couldn't imagine it. Then again, he remembered how distant her father was when he and Becca had been friends as teens.

But her mother had been kind and loving.

He also knew the elder Starkes, Becca's Aunt Julianna and Uncle Ross, and how loving and giving they were. They'd had their tough times with Julianna's cancer and other things, but they'd fought through them and come out stronger on the other side. Becca's mother was Ross Starke's sister. How could she treat her daughter like this?

Becca drew in another breath. "What about your parents?"

"What about them?"

"You haven't said much and I haven't really asked. I know you weren't super close to them when we were teens, but have things changed since then?"

"Not much." He shrugged. "They kind of do their thing and I do mine. Right now they're on a three-month-long road trip around the US."

"Did they even come home when you got shot?"

"They did."

"Oh, good."

"They love me, they just don't know what to do with me and never did. My mother was forty-eight when I came along—a modern medical surprise. So they're more like grandparents than parents, I guess."

She frowned. "Does it bother you?"

"It used to. Now, I don't let it. I have friends who let me share their holidays, and I'm an honorary uncle to several awesome kids. It's good." And it was. He liked his life. At least the part that didn't consist of spying on Becca.

"Thanks for sharing. I remember you talking about them but didn't remember seeing them around much."

"That's because my aunt pretty much raised me. She was ten years younger than my mother and doted on me. I didn't suffer a traumatic childhood or anything." He paused. "At least not until you moved away. That nearly broke my heart."

She flushed. "Broke mine, too." Then she sighed. "Do you mind checking on Brody Mac and making sure that he's all right? I think I'm getting ready to fall over." She held up a hand at his move to take her arm. "Not literally. At least, not yet. I can make it inside."

"Okay. I'll meet you in the house."

Nathan watched her go, her shoulders bowed, head tilted sideways while she rubbed her right temple. His jaw tightened. He had to find out who was causing her all this trouble and grief, and he had to find out fast. Because he wasn't sure how much more Becca could take.

SEVEN

Becca walked into the kitchen and twinkling lights from the den caught her attention. "Wait a minute, what's this?"

She stepped into the room and gasped.

"You like it?" Nathan asked from behind her. She hadn't heard him follow.

"I love it." Tears welled and she sniffed. "It's fabulous. And amazing." She walked to the mantel and touched each stocking. There were three. One for her, one for Jack, and one for Brody Mac.

"Good, I'm relieved. I was afraid you'd be upset that we did it as a surprise."

"We?"

"Brody Mac and me."

Becca turned back to the stockings. "I just need to rearrange these."

"Oh. Okay. Sorry, did I put them in the wrong order?"

"Nope, they're in the right order, there just needs to be room for one more." She moved them down and left space at the end.

Nathan lifted a brow. "For who?"

"You." She slipped into his arms to rest her cheek

against his chest. "Thank you, Nathan. It's a lovely surprise. So thoughtful and special."

"You're special." His husky voice sent shivers dancing along her nerve ends. "Becca, I…"

"What is it?"

He stared at her a moment longer, then lowered his head until his lips touched hers. A light feather of a touch. Her breathing ceased. Thinking stopped. The world tilted.

And in that sweet moment, everything was right. No one was trying to kill her, her financial problems faded to nothing and she simply reveled in the moment, taking comfort in his embrace.

Then he cleared his throat and stepped back. "I'll just…ah…see what Brody Mac's up to and be right back, okay?"

She nodded with a frown, confused, but not wanting to question his sudden emotional withdrawal. At least not out loud. "Sure."

Nathan left and she took one last look at her beautiful den, decorated with lights, ornaments—and love. She felt loved for the first time in a very long time and it was a wonderful feeling. And so was Nathan's way of offering comfort. The fact that he kissed her was surprising. Her reaction to it was stunning. Should she ask him about it or pretend it never happened? What was the etiquette in this type of situation? Something to ponder for sure.

She went back into the kitchen to grab a carton of orange juice from the refrigerator. She could use a little sugar boost. When she saw the fully stocked shelves, she gaped. What—? Who—? When—?

Sabrina. It had to be. Clay's wife liked to mother Becca almost as she liked to mother her own four children. As soon as she hung up with Clay, she must have pulled items from her own food inventory and brought them over.

It was almost enough for Becca to fully forgive Clay for doing his job. She grimaced at that thought and inspected the food.

There was hamburger meat, pork chops and chicken. On the shelf below, Sabrina had placed potatoes, corn on the cob, peas, carrots, tomatoes, three heads of lettuce and other herbs, all grown in the garden she tended with her talented green thumb.

Gratitude filled Becca. She leaned her head against the open door. *Thank you, Sabrina. Thank you, God, for friends—now family—like Sabrina.* It occurred to Becca that maybe God was listening and while He wasn't removing all the bad stuff happening, at least He was providing support and help to get through it. Like Sabrina and Nathan and others. And even Clay.

She poured her glass of orange juice and pulled her pill bottle from the cabinet. After shaking out two, she hesitated and put one back in the bottle. She swallowed the other and then made six bacon, lettuce and tomato sandwiches.

Jack nudged his food bowl over to her and sat.

She laughed and filled it up. She loved the dog she'd raised from a puppy. He was only two years old and she'd worked hard at training him. He'd responded like a champ. Smart and eager to please, he loved her as much as she did him.

Becca pulled her phone from her pocket and dialed Sabrina's number.

"Hi, Becca, how are you?"

"Hey. I don't even know how to say thank you."

"I'm guessing you found the food."

The smile in her friend's voice triggered her own. "I found it and I'm so grateful. Thank you."

"You're welcome. When Clay called and told me what happened and how shook up you were—and I don't blame you!—I couldn't just sit here and do nothing, but I've got the munchkins today so I didn't want them running around underfoot. But I could provide food for you to cook whenever you were ready for it."

"And I'm putting it to good use right now."

"Please let me know if there's anything else I can do to help. I can come clean stalls or whatever."

"I think it's better if you don't come around here anymore. At least not until whoever is after me is caught."

"I wouldn't let that keep me away, but I won't push. Please be careful, Becca."

"I am."

She hung up and went back to preparing the sandwiches, thinking that no matter how much was going wrong in her life right now, she was still blessed.

The screen door slammed just as she finished up the last sandwich. Jack ran to the door and she smiled when she heard Nathan greeting the animal. The dog didn't linger but returned to his bowl.

While Jack munched on his food, Nathan went to the sink to wash his hands. He spied the sandwiches and looked at her with a smile. "You remembered."

"I took a chance it was still your favorite."

"Thanks, but you didn't have to go to all that trouble."

"No trouble." It was such a simple thing and she was happy to do something to express her appreciation for everything he'd done for her. "And you're welcome. You can also thank Sabrina. She brought the groceries."

He took two of the sandwiches then helped himself to some chips and a bottle of water.

They sat down together at the table.

"Brody Mac will be in shortly," Nathan said. "He was brushing down the last horse when I left him."

"He really is good help. I wish his father could see his worth. Not just as a hired hand, but simply because he's a human being with feelings and a ton of love in his heart."

"People like MacDougal are just wired wrong, I guess. Not that they come into the world like that, but something happens along the way during their lives that just sends them down the wrong path."

"Do you think there's hope that they can get back on the *right* path?"

He gave her a sad smile. "There's hope. As long as there's God, there's hope."

"Yeah. Thanks for that reminder."

The screen door opened and Brody Mac appeared. "I'm all done, Becca."

"Great. I've made you some sandwiches. Why don't you have a seat and join us?"

The big man shuffled his feet on the scuffed hardwood floor. "No, thanks. I want to go back to the bunkhouse and watch the football game. Is that okay?"

"Of course."

Becca started to get up to make him a plate, but Nathan placed a hand on her arm. "I've got this."

"Oh. Okay. Thanks."

When Brody Mac walked to the door, armed with three sandwiches, a bag of chips and three bottles of water, she watched him go—and said a silent prayer for his family. She smiled. It seemed she was doing more and more of that lately and it felt good. And right.

Then she frowned.

Nathan sat down next to her once again. "What is it?"

"Is he safe here? Should I make him leave and not come back until this is all over?"

Nathan hesitated. "He's not the target, you are. Then again, you don't want him becoming collateral damage."

"No, I definitely don't want that." She rubbed her eyes. "I'll think about it. I'm afraid if I ask him to stay away for a while, it would hurt his feelings. He won't understand and will translate that into I'm saying he did something wrong. And if I tell him that because I'm in danger and that he'll be in danger if he's around me, he'll camp out on my doorstep thinking to protect me."

Nathan grimaced. "Tough decision."

Becca shook her head. "And the truth is, while Brody Mac is a great guy with a huge heart, he can be sneaky when it suits his purposes. I'm sure he's learned the behavior from his father. If his father tells him to stay put, Brody Mac simply leaves to avoid further abuse. Nothing malicious or mean, part of it is his survival instinct. The other part is him trying to be helpful even it if it means being sneaky about it."

"How's that?"

"Once I told him he had to stay out of the bunkhouse while I was having the roof fixed. He snuck in anyway and I found him on the roof trying to nail down some shingles."

"Thinking he was helping and putting himself in danger."

"Exactly. So," she bit her lip then sighed, "I think it's best not to ask him to stay away. I would rather know he was on the property so I can be alert and looking out for him than be worried he was going to sneak on and I won't know it. Does that make sense?"

"Yes. All right. We'll just have to do our best to make sure he doesn't get caught in the middle."

"Right."

"Why don't you go to bed? You look done in."

"It's the pain pill. I think it's kicking in."

His phone dinged and lights swept across the front of the house. Becca stiffened.

He rose and went to the window to look out. Then he turned to Becca. "The cavalry is here."

Becca met his friends, three off-duty officers from Nashville who had dropped everything to come to Nathan's side simply because he'd asked them to. Nathan made the introductions in the kitchen of her home. "This is Joey Bartells, Miranda Ewing and Carson Grainger."

"Thank you all for coming," Becca said. "I can't tell you how much I appreciate it."

Joey dipped his head and shot her a smile. "Nathan explained the situation and we decided we had to help. So, glad to do it."

Carson and Miranda nodded their agreement.

Nathan motioned for them to follow him. "Come on, I'll show you around. Joey and Carson, you're in the bunkhouse so bring your bags. Miranda, you're here in the main house with Becca."

Becca smiled. "I'll show you your room."

Once the officers were settled and had their assignments from Nathan, Becca allowed herself to breathe for the first time in weeks.

Nathan's friends could stay for two days and then they'd have to be back at work. She just prayed they could catch the guy in the time allotted. She wouldn't hold her breath, but she couldn't help the little nugget of hope that buried itself in her heart.

In spite of Sabrina's generous food gift, Becca would need to run to the grocery store if she was going to feed everyone. She'd have to do that tomorrow. For now, she'd sleep. She hoped. The effects of the pill were really kicking in, and now that she felt safe, her adrenaline crash was nearby.

But first...

She pulled out her phone, took a deep breath and dialed her mother's number. It rang four times then went to voice mail. Becca let her breath out slowly. "Hi, Mom. I..." What should she say? "I'd love to talk to you if you'll call me back. I miss you." She hung up and swiped a few stray tears. She was so over crying.

After showering and slipping into a pair of flannel pants and long sleeved T-shirt, she climbed into bed and closed her eyes.

Becca had no idea what time it was when she opened her eyes to the sun streaming through her window—she just knew she'd had the best night's sleep since... forever. Jack, who'd spent the night at the foot of her bed, lifted his head and yawned. Then he hopped down and walked out of her room. No doubt he needed to go out. The doggy door had been one of the best chunks of money she'd spent.

Not the least bit in a hurry, she sat up and stretched—and noticed her Bible on the nightstand. Since the accident, she'd had trouble concentrating and hadn't read it in a while. This morning, she opened it and found her eyes landing on Deuteronomy 31:6. "Be strong and courageous. Do not be afraid or terrified because of them, for the Lord your God goes with you; he will never leave you nor forsake you."

She whispered the verse again and let it burrow deep

into her heart. "Thank you for sending, Nathan, God. I know he's here because of you."

Placing the Bible back on the nightstand, she stood and stretched carefully, taking a physical inventory. Not too bad. She then lowered herself to the rug to do her daily back exercises.

When she finished, Becca threw herself into getting ready for the day. Just before going down to find some breakfast, she looked out of her bedroom window to see someone below.

One of Nathan's friends faithfully patrolling the grounds. She thought it was Joey who had a slightly slimmer build than Carson. Yes, she was glad he was there, she just hated the reason he *needed* to be there.

When she walked into the kitchen, she found Nathan at the table with Clay. "Hey guys, what's going on?"

Clay looked up. "I stopped by to let you know that we tracked down Jeff MacDougal. I asked him about the words y'all had yesterday, but he said that's all it was. Just words."

"And you believe him?"

"I don't know, Becca. I want to blame everything on him and be done with it because I want this to be over for you, but then again, I can't arrest him on just a wish, you know? I've got no proof."

"I know. And I sure don't want you to arrest the wrong person. That's not going to help anyone."

"Exactly. I questioned some of the people who were around while you were in the shop, and no one saw the truck follow you from the therapist's office."

"Well, no one had any reason to pay any particular attention, I guess. I'd like to think the whole thing was an accident, but I know it wasn't."

"Come back to reality, cousin. The guy shot at you

and denial isn't going to help us figure out who's trying to kill you."

She ran a hand over her eyes. "I know. I know."

"I talked to Billy over at the lab in Nashville first thing this morning. He's got your car in the lineup but was willing to do a quick check on the brake line. Said it looked like someone sliced it."

Becca swallowed hard and walked over to the coffeepot to pour a cup. "I'm shocked." *Not.* "So what now?"

"You don't go anywhere alone and you keep your back against a solid surface."

Becca nodded, thankful for the presence of these men and their willingness to take everything so seriously. She'd do her best to hide her frustration. For now.

Her phone buzzed and she answered reluctantly, not anxious to hear more bad news. Someone else calling to pull a horse from her barn? More lessons to cancel? She let out a slow breath. "Priceless Riding. How can I help you?"

"Is this Rebecca Price?"

"It is."

"My name's Ray Foster. I hear you're boarding horses at your place and I need a stall. Do you have room?"

For a moment Becca almost couldn't speak.

"You there?"

"Ah, yes, yes. I do have a stall available. Would you like to come take a look?"

"I sure would. Are you available this afternoon around two o'clock?"

"Two o'clock is perfect. Thanks. But I need to tell you what's been going on around here." She had to be honest. No sense in wasting his time or hers if it was going to scare him off. She filled him in.

"I see," he said at the end of her narrative. Well, I'm not so worried about it. I still want to come take a look."

"Thank you, then. I'll see you soon."

She hung up and drew a relieved breath.

"Good news?" Nathan asked.

"Yes. I've got another boarder. I guess he's not from around here and hasn't been scared off by the baseless rumors circulating." She shot a pointed look at Clay but couldn't put any heat into it. He'd helped save her life yesterday. "And yes, I filled him in on everything that's been going on. He said it didn't matter as long his horse is taken care of."

Clay stood. "Good. I'm glad for you." He paused. "Are you going to be around for Christmas?"

She raised a brow. "Where else would I be?"

"Mom and Dad's? Everyone's going to be there this year, including Amber and Lance."

Amber, his sister who'd been a CIA operative, much to her family's surprise, had married Lance Goode, an old family friend and one of the deputies in Wrangler's Corner. Together, they'd adopted Sam, a six-year-old autistic boy, who'd been a part of Amber's last case. Becca loved all three of them and would love to see them.

"I think your parents are going to be there, as well."

Becca sucked in an audible breath then let it out on a low laugh. "Then that could be pretty awkward if I show up. I may just stay here and hang out with the horses."

Clay frowned. "Don't do that. You guys have to make up someday."

"Yes. Someday." She left it at that. She'd left a message on her mother's phone and still hadn't received a call back. That spoke volumes. Her mother always returned her phone calls in a timely manner. Waves of pain washed over her. She'd been so close to her mother, but when her father issued the ultimatum—to choose between him or their daughter—she'd chosen him.

"All right, then," Clay said. "What's on your agenda for today?"

Becca shrugged. "Just a quick run to the grocery store. Sabrina brought a good bit of groceries, but I don't know that it'll be enough to feed three extra mouths for a couple of days."

"I'll get Sabrina to do it and I'll bring it out here for you. No sense in leaving this nice protection Nathan's managed to line up for you."

"I hate to bother her."

"It's not a bother. Mom's got the kids for the day. Sabrina didn't have anything more than a haircut and grocery shopping planned. Adding your list to hers won't take her but an extra ten minutes. And bringing it out to you isn't a big deal, either. I'll do it while I'm making my rounds."

"If you're sure."

"I'm sure."

Becca nodded. "All right. Let me write down what I need and get some cash out of my bedroom."

It only took her a couple of minutes to finish the list and hand him the cash.

He pushed the items into the front pocket of his uniform. "Think about Christmas."

Becca forced a smile. "I'll think about it."

After another long look at her, Clay left and Nathan stood. "You're welcome to come to Christmas dinner with my family if you want."

She smiled. "Thanks." His parents were sweet. Older, but kind even if they were a bit self-focused. "We'll see what happens between now and then."

"Are you ready to get to work?" he asked.

"Ready when you are."

* * *

Two days had passed without another incident—discounting two more boarders who took their horses to another barn. All in all, it was very quiet around the ranch.

While the lack of violence pleased Nathan, it also frustrated him. And Becca's obvious discouragement tore at his heart. He wanted to fix this for her and was doing his best, but it just wasn't good enough.

And now his police officer buddies had taken off two hours ago, although they'd departed with promises to return at the end of their next shifts should they be needed.

Ray Foster's horse had been delivered—along with the first month's boarding fees—and now seemed content in his new stall.

Zeb planned to be out that day to give him the once-over and a couple of vaccinations he was behind on.

Nathan hadn't had another chance to check out Becca's office. Truly, if there were drugs being run on the property, he couldn't figure out how it was being done or who could be doing it. There were no unsupervised strangers, no suspicious deliveries. Nothing. And there'd been no more odd things happening at night or attempts on anyone's life.

The one reason for the sudden quiet on the ranch *had* to be the extra security. And now that it was gone, Nathan knew he'd have to be hypervigilant. A thought occurred to him and he dialed Clay's number.

"Hello?"

"Hey, I have a question for you."

"All right. Ask."

"Have you vetted everyone who has access to the ranch? To the barn and the other buildings on the land?"

"As far as background checks?"

"Yes. My reason for asking is there are a few people who come on this land on a regular basis. If there are drugs being delivered around here, it's got to be one of them."

Clay's sigh came through the line. "Yeah. I did all that already. You've got delivery people, the regular lesson folks who are there on a weekly basis, you've got people calling and asking for a tour of the place because they're *thinking* of boarding their horse there. And then you've got the vet, the farrier, the boarders, those who lease some of the horses. The place has people coming and going all the time."

"I noticed that, but it has to be someone who has regular access to it. Someone Becca wouldn't think twice about being there." But that was everyone who showed up. Anyone could be the culprit. *If* there were drugs being run on the property. He still wasn't convinced that was the case. "So let me just get one thing clear. No drugs have been found on the property."

"Nope."

"All you had to go on was the cell phone with Becca's number in it."

"And the text."

"Yes. And the text."

"Clay, this is all circumstantial evidence."

"I know. But it's the closest thing I've got to a lead and I have to chase it as far as I can."

"And you still think Becca's involved?"

Clay hesitated. "Not really. Not in the sense that she's guilty or hiding something. But, as circumstantial as it is, it still comes back to her property. And the fact that someone is trying to kill her tells me I'm close—and she's probably not involved other than being a victim."

He paused. "Or they want to get rid of her because she knows too much."

"Yeah, that's not it. Becca's nerves are close to shredding. I'm convinced she's not involved in whatever's going on. She's in danger."

"I really want you to be right about that, so stay close to her, Nathan. I'm worried."

"I know the feeling." He hung up and stretched his arms over his head, trying to loosen up his tight muscles. He'd noticed now that the extra security had left, Becca's tension was once again at epic heights and rolling off of her in waves.

She appeared from around the side of the barn. "Zeb's on his way."

"Sounds good. I have a question for you."

"Sure."

"Who would benefit from buying this place should it go up for sale?"

She paused. Then shrugged. "I don't know. I guess just about anyone who wanted a pretty piece of property located about an hour outside of Nashville that's already set up for horses."

He sighed. "There's no oil, there's no real estate potential, like for someone who wanted to build a highrise or a resort. So I don't think it's anything like that."

"I don't, either."

"This seems more personal. Like you're in the way—or someone simply has it in for you for some reason."

"Yes."

"And it all started with your fall from the horse."

She nodded and frowned.

"Do you have a will?"

"Of course."

"Who gets this barn if you're dead?"

"You mean other than the bank?"

"Yes."

She shrugged. "Aaron and Zoe. They love the animals and would take care of them. They'd do something good with the place or sell it to someone who would. And I don't believe for a second that they have anything to do with all the trouble I'm having."

"No. I don't, either. And you don't remember anything else from the day of your fall?"

"No. Not really. It comes in snatches. I remember earlier that day being in the barn and working with the horses, waiting on Christine, my trainer. Pete seemed fine. After that, things get fuzzy. I don't actually remember this part, but Christine said that she and I rode out to the pasture, and then Pete just went kind of crazy. She said he started bucking, spinning and running in circles." She pressed her fingers against her eyes. "I have flashes of that last part. I remember the fear. I remember someone screaming. Christine said it was her telling me to jump. She said it was over quickly but seemed to go on forever." She gave a low laugh devoid of humor and shook her head. "I keep thinking I'm missing something." She blew out a breath and rubbed her temples. "I know I am. There are gaps that simply won't close. There's something that's just on the edge of my memory, but I can't grasp it and pull it in to examine it."

"Was anyone else here at the ranch that day? Besides you and Christine?"

"Earlier in the day when I was in the barn, Sharon was here, but she left after she rode Lady Lou. I distinctly remember her leaving because she asked if we could have lunch the next week. The farrier was there that morning, but other than that, it was a slow day.

That's why I scheduled the lesson with Christine when I did." She started to shake her head then stopped. "But wait. It seems like there was someone else."

"Who?"

"I... I don't know." She could almost see the person. But it was like looking through a foggy glass. Then a sharp pain sliced through her head and she gasped.

He laid a hand on her arm and squeezed her bicep. "Becca? Are you all right?"

"Yes. Just...a memory. I think."

"Of what?"

"I don't know." Another pain hit her and she winced. "I have to stop trying to remember."

"Can you ask Christine if there was anyone else at the barn that day? We'll talk to Sharon and the farrier, but if there was anyone else, we need to know."

"Sure." The pain receded quickly. More quickly than it ever had before, and she took heart that it was a sign she was healing.

She pulled her phone from her back pocket and texted the question. "She teaches at different barns so it may take her a bit to get back to me if she's in the middle of a lesson."

"That's fine."

The sound of an engine caught his attention, and he turned to see an old blue pickup pull into the circular drive.

She pressed a hand to her head. "That's Zeb."

"I'm just going to start cleaning the tack," Nathan said. "I noticed it needed it."

She flushed. "Yes. I haven't been able to keep up with it like I need to, and Brody Mac doesn't have the best fine motor skills."

"No problem. It's a good thinking chore."

She started off to meet Zeb who was climbing out of his truck. Before stepping into the barn, Nathan turned to watch her graceful movements. Just looking at her right now, he'd never know she had a sprained back that hurt her almost all the time. His heart gave a little lurch of longing. He still cared about her, still wanted to explore the possibility of... What? Something. The possibility of there being a "them?"

Yes. He definitely wanted that. But how did she feel about the good-looking vet?

She stopped in front of Zeb and he said something. Nathan caught the words, "new horse" and "settled." He moved closer in time to hear Becca say, "Yes. Do you know him?"

"He's a friend of mine. I convinced him there was nothing to the drug rumors, and he said he'd give you a try."

Becca reached out to hug the man and Nathan stiffened. Then he gave himself a mental shake. They were friends. He'd done something kind for her and she was simply thanking the man. Becca was a hugger.

Still, Nathan scowled at the handsome vet. He couldn't help but wish she'd settled for a handshake.

EIGHT

Zeb was busy with the remaining horses in the barn. She pondered the fact that he sure was out at the barn a lot, but then again, it didn't take a genius to figure out he was interested in her. And truthfully, if Nathan hadn't shown back up in her life, she might have given Zeb a second look. Maybe.

Then again, maybe not. She was so busy with the barn and trying to make a living that romance was definitely at the bottom of her priority list.

Until she'd seen Nathan Williams again and realized that while he'd been her best friend in high school, friendship wasn't the only thing she felt. That crazy spark that had arched between them when the terror of her attack in the barn had faded was still there in the forefront of her mind. Not to mention the kiss. A soft kiss. Comforting and healing. But with the potential for so much more.

She rubbed her eyes. Nathan was the best thing to happen to her in a long time and she was grateful. She just wished the circumstances surrounding their reunion were different.

Because right now, Becca wanted to run away from the turmoil that had become her life. Run away and not look back. But she wasn't that kind of person. She'd learned early on that if she wanted something, she had to stand up, grab hold and take it.

Becca slipped into a shady little area surrounded by bricks. One side of the structure had been cleared away so it had three walls with ninety-degree corners. She thought the bricks might be the remains of an old brick fireplace once upon a time. Either from a house that burned down years ago or someone had had an outdoor area.

The Updikes had created this little nook that was a good place to simply sit and soak in the beauty of the property around her. It was off to the side of the house where the land sloped upward before it turned into a copse of dense trees. A shallow lazy creek flowed at the bottom of the space.

Becca loved the cozy feel of sitting inside it, especially when she was feeling overwhelmed.

Such as right now.

Her phone rang. Christine. "Hi. Thanks for calling me back."

"Sure. What's up?"

"The day I fell off the horse, was there anyone else here on the ranch? You know my memories are fuzzy, and it seems like there was another person here, but I can't remember."

"I didn't see any—oh wait!"

"What?"

"There was the guy that stopped by to ask about lessons for his daughter."

"Who? I don't remember that."

"Think he said his name was Larry something. Black? Brown? Bowen. That's it. Larry Bowen."

"I don't have his name anywhere."

"No. Think he was just a drive-by. You gave him some information and he left, but it delayed our lesson a bit."

Becca looked at the blue sky and huddled deeper into her heavy coat. While the sun was out, the wind was chilly. "Did you tell the cops any of this?"

"No. No one asked. Why would the cops need to know? Your fall was an accident, right?"

"Right. Of course it was. I'm just still trying to remember the details from that day. They're nagging at me, but I just can't seem to grab them. Thanks for getting back to me."

"Of course. Anything else?"

"Not unless you remember something else."

"Sorry. I'll think on it some more and call you if I do."

"That would be great."

"Talk to you later."

She hung up and leaned back. Larry Bowen. The name meant nothing to her. But it might to Clay who could figure out who the guy was. Probably just a parent looking for a riding school. She had people stop by on a regular basis to get information about lessons, boarding and trail rides—or at least she had before the rumors started.

That thought brought her back to the fact that someone wanted her off this ranch. And the only person she could think of who might go to these lengths to get her to leave was her father. The thought pained her and she wanted to immediately dismiss the idea, but she simply couldn't.

Then again, what about Brody Mac's father? He probably didn't mind her running her ranch, but he sure didn't like her allowing his son to find refuge there.

Would he go so far as to kill her to stop it? Had he cut the brake line on her truck?

She shuddered.

A footstep behind her sent her scrambling for her rifle, ignoring the pain in her back the sudden movement provoked. She spun only to see Nathan standing on one of the large rocks that bordered the river.

"You scared me."

"You need to be scared. What do you think you're doing going off on your own?"

"It's my land. I shouldn't have to be worried about being on it." She heard the petulance in her voice and winced.

"Well…" he said.

"Well, what?"

"That's just stupid."

She laughed, but the sound lacked humor. "I know that."

"You know that, huh? Well, good. You had me worried there for a minute."

Becca sighed. "I just can't stay cooped up waiting for him to strike again. My job, my livelihood, is entirely outdoors. If I have to stay indoors, I might as well pack everything up and *give* up. I *have* to be out here or I'll lose everything."

"True."

"And besides, I have my back up against a brick wall per Clay's recommendation."

"I noticed. You actually picked a pretty good spot. Mind if I join you?"

"Sure."

He took a seat beside her and mimicked her posture. Back against the rock, knees raised and forearms resting on top of them. "This is not too bad. Bricks and rocks on either side of you and the wall behind you. It's like a mini shelter. Not bad. Kind of the way a cop would think."

"Thanks."

"It's not worth your life, Becca," he said softly. "Some things are worth dying for. A lot of things, actually, but not this."

She sighed. "I know. You're right, of course. And that's one thing I'm trying so hard to figure out."

"What's that?"

"Well, first off, who is Larry Bowen?"

He blinked. "I don't know? Why?"

"Christine said he was the man who was here the day of the accident, that he'd wanted information about riding lessons."

"The day of the accident, huh?"

"Yep."

"I'll text Clay and ask him to look into him, but what can you tell me about him?"

"Nothing. I don't remember him. I mean, I do, but I don't. Like it's just a fog that I can't quite see through."

He frowned. "Okay. We'll figure it out."

"Is Zeb finished yet?" she asked.

"Yep. Sent him on his way about ten minutes ago and thought I'd come find you. So, what else are you thinking about?"

"Life. And God."

"What about it—and Him?"

"You'll think I'm silly."

"No way."

She sighed. "You know my parents."

"Hmm. Somewhat. Not really well. It's not like we were hanging out with them when we were in high school."

"That's true, but you know enough to know that they've always pampered me, given me everything I've ever wanted."

"Yeah."

"They even supported my horse addiction." She shot him a small smile. "But I learned at an early age that anything my father gave me came with expectations—or strings."

He raised a brow. "What do you mean?"

"Did you know when I went to college, I actually got counseling? To learn how to deal with my feelings about my parents? Mostly my father, but I had some resentment toward my mother even though I know she loved me."

He gripped her fingers. "I didn't know that."

"Well, I don't exactly go around advertising the fact, but yes, I did."

"Was the counseling helpful?"

"Extremely." She turned to look at him for the first time since he'd joined her. "Lisa, my counselor, became a good friend once I was no longer a patient. I miss her."

"She's in Nashville?"

"Yes. We have lunch every once in a while when I find myself in Nashville." She pursed her lips. "Which hasn't been very often, unfortunately."

"So what did you learn about yourself and your feelings?"

"Exactly what I was saying. That everything my father does is for a reason. He never does anything just from the goodness of his heart. If he gives you something, he expects something in return."

"Ouch. Like what?"

She shrugged. "It could be something as simple as loyalty. His version of it, not Webster's."

FREE Merchandise is 'in the Cards' for you!

Dear Reader,

We're giving away FREE MERCHANDISE!

Seriously, we'd like to reward you for reading this novel by giving you **FREE MERCHANDISE** worth over **$20** retail. And no purchase is necessary!

You see the Jack of Hearts sticker above? Paste that sticker in the box on the Free Merchandise Voucher inside. Return the Voucher today... and we'll send you Free Merchandise!

Thanks again for reading one of our novels—and enjoy your Free Merchandise with our compliments!

Pam Powers

Pam Powers

P.S. Look inside to see what Free Merchandise is **"in the cards"** for you!

We'd like to send you two free books like the one you are enjoying now. Your two books have a combined cover price of over $10 retail, but they are yours to keep absolutely FREE! We'll even send you 2 wonderful surprise gifts. You can't lose!

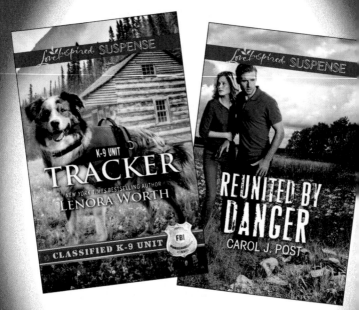

REMEMBER: Your Free Merchandise, consisting of **2 Free Books** and **2 Free Gifts**, is worth over $20 retail! No purchase is necessary, so please send for your Free Merchandise today.

Get TWO FREE GIFTS!

We'll also send you 2 wonderful FREE GIFTS (worth about $10 retail), in addition to your 2 Free books!

Visit us at:
www.ReaderService.com

YOUR FREE MERCHANDISE INCLUDES...
2 FREE Books **AND** 2 FREE Mystery Gifts

FREE MERCHANDISE VOUCHER

2 FREE BOOKS and **2 FREE GIFTS**

Please send my Free Merchandise, consisting of
2 Free Books and **2 Free Mystery Gifts**.
I understand that I am under no obligation to buy
anything, as explained on the back of this card.

❏ I prefer the regular-print edition
153/353 IDL GMWD

❏ I prefer the larger-print edition
107/307 IDL GMWD

Please Print

FIRST NAME

LAST NAME

ADDRESS

APT.# CITY

STATE/PROV. ZIP/POSTAL CODE

NO PURCHASE NECESSARY!

SLI-N17-FFM17

(vertical left margin) ▶ Detach card and mail today. No stamp needed. ▶

© 2017 HARLEQUIN ENTERPRISES LIMITED. Printed in the U.S.A.

READER SERVICE—Here's how it works:

"Ah. Meaning, you do whatever he decrees because he's given to you."

"Or done something for you. Yep."

"I'm glad you can see that's not healthy."

"I can. I've also come to understand that it's okay that I want to live my life the way I want to live it. I'm not obligated to live the life my parents planned for me. Only the life God has for me. And that brings me back to Him. I know He's not like my father. He loves me unconditionally—a concept that I still try to wrap my brain around sometimes. But I'm also having a hard time reconciling that with all the trouble He's allowing to happen on the ranch. If I'm doing what He wants me to do, why is it so hard?"

"I get what you're saying. I've questioned that a time or two myself. But all of this didn't catch Him by surprise."

"I know that, too. Which is why I'm trying to roll with it—and talk to Him again with the faith that He hears me even if I don't always hear His answer or see the full picture of what He's got in mind." She drew in a deep breath, closing her eyes on the heady scent of the nearby lake. "I love this place. It's a good thinking place."

"Could be good for that, or…"

"Or what?" She opened her eyes and turned to face him.

He lifted a hand and placed it at the base of her neck. "Or it could be a good kissing place."

Her heart thudded. "Kissing place? For who?"

He grinned. "Who do you think?"

For *them*? He wanted to kiss her again?

And then his head lowered and his lips covered hers. She didn't move for a moment, simply savoring the feel of him so close, his warmth next to hers, his scent surrounding her. A combination of sweat and soap. He definitely wanted to kiss her again. She loved it.

She enjoyed the intimate moment, soaking in the brief blip in time where she felt completely safe. And then he deepened the kiss, pulling her closer.

Nathan. She was kissing Nathan. Like really kissing him. Not just a soft meeting of the lips, but a real kiss that could last forever as far as she was concerned. It was weird…and wonderful. She leaned into him and sighed. His hand slid from her neck to the back of her head and then he was pulling back. Becca moved her hands to grip the front of his shirt and then opened her eyes to find him staring down at her. "Why did you do that?" she whispered.

"It seemed like a good idea at the time."

"Oh." She paused, then nodded. "It was definitely a good idea."

The corners of his eyes creased with his smile. She'd never noticed that before.

"Really?" he said.

"Uh-huh."

"I've been known to come up with a good idea or two occasionally."

The creases disappeared.

"Then why are you frowning?" she asked.

"Because it might not have been the best idea after all."

"Um…why?"

"Because there are things you don't know, things I probably should tell—"

The crack of a rifle shattered the moment.

NINE

Nathan yanked her to the back of the brick shelter and covered her with his body. "You have your phone? Please tell me you have it."

"Yes." Her voice quivered on the one word and fury flooded him. She didn't deserve this. And she didn't deserve to have him kissing her when he wasn't being completely honest with her.

"Call Clay."

She shifted and he rolled, keeping her behind him while he faced the opening with his weapon aimed in the direction he thought the bullet had come from. She'd picked a great spot as far as cover, but as long as someone was shooting, they were definitely trapped.

"He's not answering. I'm going to call 911."

"Do it."

Then her phone rang. "It's Clay," she said, and slapped the device to her ear. "Someone's shooting at us on the ranch. Around back. We're trapped and need help. Yes. Yes. Thanks. No, I won't hang up." She shivered. "He's coming."

Nathan nodded and let his eyes scan the area. Whoever was shooting at them was very good at hiding. And there were a lot of places to hide. Someone with a long-range rifle could pick them off easily if they left the shelter.

"He said Trent is out this way and should be here soon."

"Soon. How soon is soon?"

She lifted the phone back to her ear. "Did you hear that?" She listened a minute then said, "Trent's pulling onto the property. It'll take him about a minute to get to the house."

"I don't see the shooter," Nathan said. "There was only the one shot and then nothing."

"He's been watching," she said, "just waiting for a chance to strike again. He knew your friends were here and he laid low, let me relax a little, get a bit comfortable with nothing happening for two straight days. He waited for your friends to leave and now he's ready to pick back up in his attempts to kill me."

"It's a good theory."

"I'm not relaxing anymore," she said. "Not until this is all resolved."

"I think that's probably a good idea."

"When Clay first asked me about running drugs, I was *highly* offended, of course."

"Of course." He continued to scout the trees beyond. If the guy moved and got in a direct line of sight with the opening of their little hideaway, it's possible he could hit Nathan with a well-placed bullet. The thought made him *highly* uncomfortable.

Sirens reached his ears and he thought he saw a flash of a figure in the trees just across from where they hid. He followed the sight and heard the sound of an engine rev. A motorcycle?

Nathan gave a grunt of frustration mingled with relief. "He's gone. There's no way to catch him now."

"Are you sure?"

"Pretty sure."

Unless it was a trick to make him *think* the guy was gone. Only one way to find out. He rolled out of the hideaway and then back, waiting for the shot.

Nothing.

He did it again. Nothing. A minute passed. Then two. He heard the crunch of tires on gravel. Trent. "I think we're good." He turned to help Becca out. She rose stiffly, one hand on her lower back. "You okay?"

"Yes. Just my usual stiffness."

"Is Clay still on the phone?"

"Yes." She handed it to him.

"Clay?"

"I'm here."

"The shooter just took off on a motorcycle. I'm sure he's running the length of the property looking for a spot to hit the road that will take him back to town. Probably whatever opening he made in it to get out here. Look for the broken fence—and then let me know where it is because I'll have to get it fixed ASAP."

"Got it. I'll put out a BOLO. Is Trent there yet?"

"Yes." He could see the cruiser in the drive with the lights flashing.

"Good. Get Becca inside and keep your heads down. Keep me on the line until then."

Nathan and Becca hurried toward the house. Trent met them and followed them inside and Clay hung up. "You two okay?" Trent asked.

"We're fine," Nathan said. "Have you got someone going after the motorcycle?"

"Yeah. I heard the BOLO come through. Everyone on duty is on the lookout." The deputy shook his head. "Sorry about all the trouble you're having, Becca."

"Thanks. Me, too." Her eyes widened. "That's Zeb's truck. Thought you said he left."

"He did. At least I thought he did."

"We should probably check on him."

"I'll do it," Trent said. "Stay here."

Once the door shut behind him, Becca sank into one of the kitchen chairs and dropped her head into her hands. She sat that way for a full minute before looking up. "I have to do something."

"What?"

"I don't know. Set a trap for this person, something."

Nathan rubbed his chin. "That might not be a bad idea."

Trent stepped out of the barn and called for Becca to come in.

She hurried inside and found Zeb kneeling next to Pete. He had the horse's front left hoof propped up on his knee and was examining it.

"What is it?" Becca asked.

Zeb looked up. "Hey."

"I wasn't expecting you today. What are you doing?"

"I just wanted to take another look at his abscess. I thought it might be getting infected the last time I looked at it and treated it. But it's healed up real well." He lowered the horse's foot to the ground and stood.

"Did you hear the gunshot?"

"Yeah. Everything okay?"

Nathan frowned. "You weren't concerned enough to investigate?"

Zeb shrugged. "No, why? Gunshots are so common around here that I didn't think much of it. Was it a snake or a wolf?"

"Definitely a snake," Becca muttered. "Or a wolf in sheep's clothing."

Zeb's frown deepened. "Why do I get the feeling I should have paid more attention and been a little more concerned?"

"Someone shot at us," Nathan said.

"What?" His eyes went immediately to Becca. "Why? Are you sure? Are you okay?"

"Pretty sure. And yes, I'm fine."

"I am, too," Nathan said. "Thanks."

Zeb flushed and Becca wanted to slug Nathan for his dry comment.

Nathan ducked his head, then looked up as he cleared his throat. "Anyway, I don't guess you saw anything else."

"No, I checked the heifer, then was in here with the horses."

"All right," Clay said. "Let's wrap this up. Becca, you and Nathan go inside. Trent, come with me. We'll see if we can find the bullet."

An hour later, Becca sat at the kitchen table while Nathan and Clay discussed where to go from here. Clay had found the bullet buried in the brick wall that had protected Becca and Nathan from the gunman. "I'll get this to the lab in Nashville. Hopefully, it won't take forever to get some information back on it. I don't know who this guy is, but he's leaving evidence that can be used against him when we catch him."

Becca sighed. "Soon, I hope."

"I know it seems like it's taking a long time to figure this out, but it's only been a few days—and there's not much to go on."

"I know."

"Anything on Larry Bowen?" Nathan asked.

"Yes. He was next on my agenda to discuss with you. Looks like a troublemaker. Has a few priors for possession. We're trying to track him down but haven't had any success thus far. I'll keep you updated on that as soon as I know anything."

"Good," Nathan said.

Clay stood. "All right. You stay put. Stay inside as much as possible."

"Clay—"

He held up a hand. "I know. I get it. I understand your arguments, but the fact of the matter is, the more you're outside, the more danger you're in."

Becca rubbed her forehead. "I know that, Clay. I promise I'll do my best to stay behind some kind of protection. In the barn or in the house or…" She waved a hand. "I don't know. I'll try, though."

"I guess that's as good as I'm going to get. And I promise to send a patrol around as often as possible."

"Thanks."

Becca was grateful but wasn't going to hold her breath. She sat in silence with Nathan until she heard footsteps on the porch again.

Nathan bolted to his feet and Becca straightened.

"It's just me." Clay stepped back inside, holding a vest in his hands. He walked over and set it on the table. "It won't protect you from a head shot, but it'll keep you a lot more safe than wearing nothing."

Becca swallowed. "Okay. I'll wear it."

He looked surprised. "Good."

Clay made his way out the door once again.

A few seconds later, the sound of an engine pulling up outside caught her attention, and she went to the window to look out.

Nathan joined her and she jolted at his nearness. That

kiss was still very fresh in her mind. And on her lips. "Who is it?" he asked.

"Brody Mac's dad."

"What's he doing here?"

"I don't know. I was just getting ready to find out. Clay and Trent are getting ready to leave, as is Zeb. They're all at their vehicles watching MacDougal. I think it's safe to step outside."

He handed her the vest. "Not without this."

"Right." Nathan helped her put it on and adjust it.

"It's heavy," she said.

"That's the point. You want it to stop any bullets that might come your way."

"Right." She pulled her heavy coat over it and then walked out onto the porch. "Hello, Mr. MacDougal. What can I do for you?"

"I came to get Brody Mac."

She frowned at him. "I'm not sure where he is."

"Then go find him."

She crossed her arms, then dropped them when the bulk prevented her from doing so comfortably. "You know, it's awfully convenient for you to show up just now."

He rubbed a dirty hand over his chin. "What're you talking about, girlie?"

"Someone just took a shot at Nathan and me out behind the house. You know anyone who'd want to do that?"

"A shot at you? What are you saying?"

What a thick-headed man. "That someone just tried to kill us."

He frowned. "Probably someone you were too interfering with. Now where's my boy?"

"Your concern overwhelms me, MacDougal," Clay

said. "And you don't have any reason to keep Brody Mac from being here."

"You stay outta this. This ain't none of your concern."

The sound of a moped reached Becca during their exchange and she saw Brody Mac heading down the drive.

His father didn't seem to notice.

"Why are you so intent on keeping him away from here?" she asked. She'd stall and let Brody Mac get as far away as possible.

"Because you got drugs on this place! I don't want him caught up in that mess."

She stamped a foot. "I don't have drugs here! And you've been harassing him about not coming here long before those rumors got started, so why don't you tell the truth for once?"

His face turned red and she thought she saw a few tendrils of smoke curl from his ears. He started toward her and Nathan stepped forward. "That's close enough."

Becca pulled Nathan back and faced the man who'd stopped at Nathan's words. But he pointed a nicotine-stained finger at her. "You need to stay out of other people's lives. You're messing with my family and I won't stand for that. If you keep putting your nose where it don't belong, you're going to regret it!"

"What are you going to do? Shoot at me?"

"I just might, girlie, I just might. Now you keep to yours and leave mine alone."

He climbed back in his truck, and with a crunch of tires on the gravel spun around the drive and headed away from the ranch. Her head started to pound. The stress of the day was definitely catching up to her. She raised her hands to massage her temples.

Clay sighed and shook his head. "Sorry, Becca. I can't arrest him just because he's got a loud mouth."

"I know."

"You handled him well," Nathan said. "Stood up to him and let him know he's not going to run over you. Nice."

And he hadn't interfered in her handling of it except for the one protective move when he'd stepped in front of her. All three men had let her deal with the irascible father. But she knew they would have had her back if she'd needed them.

They were true friends. She swallowed the sudden lump in her throat. "Thanks, guys."

Nathan nodded to Clay and Trent. "Do y'all have time to come back inside for a minute? Becca said something that got me to thinking."

"What's that?" Clay asked.

"Maybe a way to catch whoever's got it in for her."

"I'm willing to listen to that plan, sure."

They all returned to the den area. Trent and Clay settled on her sofa while Nathan took the wingback chair near the fireplace.

Becca fired up the gas logs and a warm glow filled the room. She didn't use the logs often because it could get expensive, but right now, she was cold and needed comforting. And since Nathan's arms weren't available at the moment, she wrapped the fleece blanket around her shoulders and settled into the matching wingback chair opposite Nathan's.

He cleared his throat. "Becca said something about setting a trap to catch whoever's been trying to kill her. I don't know about a trap, per se, but what about if we make it look like no one is here at night? While Becca has to be here during the day, she can leave at night while we keep a constant vigil on the property. Someone awake at all times, which means sleeping in shifts. I think it might be a good idea as long as we can keep her safe."

Clay leaned forward and clasped his hands. "That's not a bad idea. How do you propose to make that happen and still make sure everyone gets enough sleep?"

For the next half hour the four of them outlined a plan to set into motion that night. Nathan wanted her completely gone from the property, but she shook her head. "No. Where would I go?"

"You could stay with Sabrina," Clay said.

"Absolutely not. Somehow, he'll know it. He's watching me, following me, keeping track of my every movement. I don't know how, whether he's got some high-powered binoculars and is sitting in a tree somewhere or what, but I won't put Sabrina and your children in danger. And that goes for the rest of the people you're getting ready to name."

Clay sighed. "What about a hotel room?"

"I can't afford it and I'm not asking you to pay for it."

Nathan scowled. "Then what if we make him think Becca's gone? Let him think she's left and not coming back for a while?"

"What do you have in mind?" Clay asked.

"Put her in a truck and drive her to the hotel. Make sure it's obvious she's checking in and then have her use the restroom in the lobby, don a disguise and then sneak out the back. I can be waiting with a truck our guy wouldn't recognize."

"Where will you get the truck?"

"I'll find one."

"He might not even fall for it and you all have gone to an awful lot of trouble," Becca said softly.

Clay held his hands between his knees and spun it while he thought. "Might not, but we can plan to do this for the next few nights and see what shakes loose. I'll try to take some time during the day to sleep and I'll make sure Trent has the time off, as well. Nathan, you get the day shift around here. Our guy probably knows you're the hired hand. He expects you to be here and working. If something happens at night, we'll wake you."

Nathan's scowl didn't lessen, but he didn't argue the plan.

Something blipped in Becca's memory. Someone in the barn. In the feed room. She could only see the back of him, but he looked familiar. "Hey, what are you doing in here?" she'd asked.

A sharp pain shot through the front of her head and she winced.

"Becca?" Nathan asked. "You okay?"

"Yes." She blinked and tried to bring the memory back. "I'm okay. I just thought I remembered something about the day of the accident, but now it's gone."

Clay's phone rang. "Excuse me for a second."

He stepped out of the room to take the call and Trent excused himself as well, leaving her alone with Nathan.

And the memory of that kiss they'd shared.

And the realization that she wouldn't mind sharing another one with him. At what point had he stopped being her former friend and newly hired hand, and started being someone she daydreamed about kissing?

She wasn't exactly sure, but while kissing Nathan was certainly enjoyable, she needed to focus on who was trying to kill her. Or them. The person didn't seem worried about collateral damage. The thought sent shivers dancing over her skin and dread straight into her heart. If anything happened to Nathan, she didn't know how she'd be able to live with herself. If she actually lived.

"Earth to Becca."

She jumped. "Oh. Sorry. Just thinking."

"About what?"

Her gaze dropped to his lips before she could stop it. She jerked her eyes away. "Ah…it doesn't matter."

He eyed her and from the glint that sparkled for a brief moment, she saw he knew exactly what she'd been thinking—the kissing parts of her thoughts anyway. Then his eyes clouded over. "All right. If you're going to be up most of the night, it's time for you to grab some shut-eye. I'll keep watch so you can rest easy."

She stood. "Thank you."

"How's your back?"

"It's hurting a bit. I'll take something to take the edge off."

Actually, it was killing her. All the jerking around and overusing it had her on the edge of tears. But there was no use crying about it.

And the fact that her mother still hadn't returned her call had nothing to do with her weepy feeling.

Okay, yes, it did.

She turned the logs off and left Nathan in the den checking his email as she walked down the hall to her bathroom. After she took her meds, she got as comfortable as possible on the bed and closed her eyes. *I miss you, Mom.* She sighed. *Please, God, let me live long enough to reconcile with my parents or at least my mom. I really don't want to die without some sort of understanding between us all. Please.*

TEN

Three nights passed with nothing. Becca stayed house-bound, staying away from the windows, not answering the door or going to the barn. Nathan was actually impressed with her determination to see the plan through. The hotel had Becca registered as a guest in room 304 if anyone decided to snoop. Since there wasn't the manpower to keep someone on the hotel room, they set up cameras to monitor the room. So far, no one had made any suspicious moves around the room.

Or the ranch.

No strange or suspicious activity, and no problems during the day. Nathan was about ready to think the person was privy to inside information and knew they were watching, waiting to spring a trap. However, they all agreed to give it two more nights and then come back together to revamp the plan.

In the meantime, with Becca trapped in the house, he had no time to slip into her office to go through her hard-copy files. The computer had turned up nothing and he expected the same for whatever was in the file cabinet next to her desk. The truth is, he didn't believe she was guilty of anything more than being in the wrong place at the wrong time, and he had no motivation to bother checking.

He told Clay so as the sun went down on the clear December evening. Clay nodded. "I'm leaning in your direction, but it wouldn't hurt to just check. At least then I can say I covered all my bases."

"Hmm. We'll see."

Clay looked around. "Glad to see she finally got around to decorating."

"She had a little help and encouragement."

Clay fell silent for a minute. "You still care for her, don't you?"

"Yes."

"But you're trying not to."

"Yep."

Clay laughed.

"It's not funny. My whole presence here has been a lie. Keeping the truth from her is killing me. I need to tell her everything."

"Yeah. I know."

"I'd tell her right now if I didn't think she'd kick me off the ranch and leave herself vulnerable to whoever's been trying to kill her."

Clay shook his head and frowned. "No, it's best to stay quiet for now. If she knows I'm the one who asked you to do this, we'll both be in the doghouse. And she'll be a sitting duck."

"So we keep our mouths shut for now. But I don't feel it's right to pursue anything with her until there's no secrets between us, you know?"

Clay nodded. "Well, if she gives you a hard time about it, you can just blame me."

"I was planning to do that anyway."

Clay snorted then shook his head. "I should have known."

"How are Sabrina and the kids?"

The besotted expression on Clay's face spoke volumes. "They're great. Sabrina is amazing and the kids are growing like crazy." Then he sighed. "I just wish I got to spend more time with them."

"I see Seth is up for the National Finals Rodeo again this year." Seth was one of Clay's younger brothers who, very successfully, traveled the rodeo circuit.

"Yep. And his wife, Tonya, is pregnant again."

"That makes their second one, doesn't it?"

"And third."

He laughed. "Twins? Seriously?"

"Yes."

"Seth's going to have to retire and stay home to help her out."

"I know. Mom's over the moon with all the grandkids. She's instructing us to keep 'em coming." Clay sighed and glanced out the window. "The sun's coming up. I guess we can call it a night. I don't know whether to be glad at the lack of excitement or frustrated."

Nathan shook his head. "I sure did think we'd have this guy by now."

"You and me both. Trent's on his way. I'm going to head home to grab some sleep. I'll be back to swap out with Trent in a few hours."

Nathan had slept until five when he'd awakened with a full adrenaline rush thinking someone had gotten to Becca. He'd known it was a dream but had raced out of the bunkhouse to find Clay sitting in the dark kitchen, sipping coffee by a night-light. Clay had lowered his weapon to the table with a scowl. "You're fortunate I didn't shoot you."

"Same here."

The two men had put their weapons away and continued their discussion in the dark. Nathan headed back to the bunkhouse to grab his shower and start his day, once again working side by side with Becca.

He couldn't say the prospect was distasteful, he just prayed it would be another uneventful day and no one shot at anyone else.

Becca had awakened about thirty minutes before the sun was supposed to rise. She'd lain in bed for ten of those thirty minutes, then rolled out from under the covers, dressed, and made a mental outline of the chores she needed to get done today.

They had a heifer that had managed to get entangled in a wad of barbed wire fence yesterday, and Zeb promised to ride out to take a look at her.

Becca knew someone had cut that part of the fence and she'd told Clay so. After examining the wire, he'd agreed. "Too bad you don't have security cams out here."

"Yeah. Too bad. I only wish I could afford that."

She yawned and walked to the window to peer out from the side through the small slit at the side. Normally she would simply open them and stare out over her land, but not this morning. Because no one could know she was in the house today. Again. Truthfully, Becca was ready to climb the walls—or run screaming across the pasture.

But she wouldn't. She'd give Clay and Nathan today and tomorrow to see if the plan would work. If not, she was going to resume her life. Albeit, with continued caution.

Tears pricked at her eyes. What if they never caught the person responsible? What would she do?

She drew in a deep breath. She'd have to sell. Period. Swallowing hard at the depressing thought, she gave one last sweeping glance over the property and sighed. Then frowned.

In the soft glow of the slow-rising sun, she spotted the barn door open. What was Nathan or Brody Mac doing up this early? Was something wrong? When Lady Lou nudged her way out of the door, Becca gasped.

Grabbing her boots, she shoved her feet into them, snatched her rifle from its resting place against the wall, and raced down the hall. "Nathan? Clay?"

No answer.

Had one of them gone into the barn and confronted her would-be killer? Did they need help?

Becca hurried out the door and saw Trent climbing out of his cruiser. "What are you doing?" he asked.

"Something's going on in the barn. Lady Lou just got out."

Becca watched the horse jog through the open gate and into the pasture. "Shut the gate, Trent, will you?"

While he did as she requested, she turned her attention to the barn. "Nathan? Brody Mac?"

"Wait for me before you go in that barn, Becca," Trent called.

She shifted from foot to foot while she waited. He finally joined her and stepped in front of her. "Why don't you go back in the house?"

"Because no one is answering me. Not Nathan or Brody Mac and with Lady Lou getting out, I'm scared one of them is hurt. I'm the one with the medical skills, so let's get in there and make sure everything—and everyone—is all right." She hesitated for a fraction of a second. "But I'll let you go first and will listen if you give me an order. Is that sufficient?"

"Fine. Stay behind me." Trent took the lead, weapon drawn.

He stepped inside the open barn door and she heard him flip the light switch. Nothing happened.

While the sun was making its way up over the horizon, it was still too dark to see inside the barn without the light.

The horse to her right seemed restless, pacing from one end of the stall to the other. Pete. "What is it, big boy?"

He came to the opening and stuck his head through. She rubbed his nose and he seemed to calm. Then he stamped his foot and threw his head up and down. Was his foot bothering him? She checked the abscess a few times since Zeb had diagnosed it and been treating it, but mostly she'd entrusted the horse's care to him while she'd been doing her own recovering. But maybe she should take a look?

A shuffle just ahead near the feed room caught her attention. Trent heard it, too, and he stepped forward, then cried out and went to his knees.

"Trent!"

Becca tried to see through the shifting shadows but couldn't figure out what had happened. And then her rifle was ripped from her fingers and a hard forearm pressed against her throat. "You should mind your own business."

Becca struggled against the man's hold. Trent rose to his feet, swaying and lifting his weapon. "Let her go."

Her captor raised his right arm and fired his weapon at Trent. Trent went down. Becca screamed.

"Police! Freeze!"

Becca's knees nearly buckled at Nathan's shout. Her attacker swung her around to face Nathan, his gun now aimed on Nathan.

Her heart pounded while her head spun and her gaze bounced between the two. The masked face and the one who'd once again come to her rescue.

"Drop it!" Nathan ordered as he ducked around the door for cover.

"I don't think so, cowboy. You drop yours or I shoot both of you."

"I'm a cop and I've got backup coming. Right now, no one's seen your face, so either drop the weapon or start running. Either way, the clock is ticking."

The weapon pressed harder against her temple, and Becca winced as pain shot through her head. She didn't bother to fight him. He was strong and had the upper hand. She would have to wait him out and then outsmart him. While praying he didn't shoot her or anyone else.

Please God, let Trent be okay.

She caught Nathan's eye. Sirens sounded in the distance. Her captor swore and shoved her to the ground. He spun and started for the back door. Nathan raced past her. "Check Trent!"

Becca dropped to the ground next to the unconscious deputy and pressed her fingers to his pulse. It beat steady and hard beneath her fingers. As the sun rose, so did the visibility in the barn. With shaking hands, Becca checked for wounds. He'd taken a bullet in the shoulder. She raced for the first aid kit she kept in her office and grabbed it from the shelf. Hurrying back to Trent's side, she snagged the scissors from the kit and cut away his shirt. Quickly, she grabbed disinfectant, bandages and tape then turned him on his side. "In and out," she whispered. But he was bleeding—a lot.

She worked almost without thinking, her movements efficient and steady while she sent up prayers for Nathan's safety. She could hear something going on outside the barn, but couldn't leave Trent just yet without worrying he'd bleed to death if she didn't care for his wound.

Trent groaned. "Wha—"

"Shh," she said. "Stay still."

"Somebody stabbed me with a hot poker. Man, that hurts." He groaned.

"I have to stop the bleeding, Trent."

"And my head. What happened?"

"This is going to sting." She disinfected the wound and Trent cried out. Then passed out again. In record time, she finished dressing both sides, front and back, and figured that would keep him for now. She heard a cry from behind the barn and fear for Nathan clawed at her.

The goose egg on the side of Trent's head needed an ice pack, but that would have to wait. All in all, she figured with time, he'd heal up as good as new.

With thanksgiving, she left him and bolted toward the back where Nathan and her attacker had disappeared.

She found them scuffling in the dirt just beyond the barn. And then Nathan managed to flip the guy onto his back and land a bone-crunching punch to the man's face.

He went still.

Nathan rolled off of him, caught his breath, then flipped the man back over to his stomach. "You got any zip ties?"

"In the barn."

"Can you get me one?"

Becca raced to grab one from the office just as the

cruisers pulled into the yard. She waved them in her direction then ran back to Nathan, worried the prisoner would wake up and start fighting again.

Once Nathan had the man's hands bound, he rolled him to his back and pulled his mask off.

Becca gasped. "That's Larry Bowen."

ELEVEN

While Lance and Clay took care of the prisoner, Nathan worked his sore jaw and decided it wasn't broken. Bowen had gotten in a good punch before Nathan had managed to take him down. But in the end, Nathan's training and expertise had come through for him, and they now had their suspect in custody with an angry-looking deputy standing guard. Lance looked ready to land a few punches on the prisoner's battered face.

An ambulance had already come and gone with Trent who had awakened again, confused and complaining of a killer headache and a shoulder that was on fire. He didn't remember Becca bandaging him up. The paramedic had looked at them and said, "He'll be all right. We'll get him to the hospital and taken care of."

Nathan nodded.

Clay helped the shooter into the back of the cruiser while Nathan and Becca watched nearby.

Lance shut the door and shook his head. "Think your troubles are over now?"

"I sure hope so," Becca said. "But I'm still bothered by the fact that he's being so quiet. Why won't he talk?"

"He's mad he got caught."

Nathan narrowed his eyes and shot a glance at Clay's

squad car. "I don't know. Most people who don't talk are scared to. He's mad, but he's scared, too. He was pretty desperate to get away."

"You think someone's not going to be happy he got caught," Clay said.

"Exactly." Nathan crossed his arms. "Thought you were going home to sleep," Nathan said.

"I guess I'll do that next month. I stopped at the office when I left here and was just getting ready to head home when your call for backup came in." Clay looked at Becca. "So that's Larry Bowen."

"Yes." She clasped her arms across her stomach. "He's the piece I've been trying to remember. As soon as I saw his face, it came back to me. Christine was right. He stopped by the day of the accident and we talked for a few minutes. He wanted some information for his daughter who was interested in taking lessons. I gave him one of my flyers and he left. Or I thought he did."

"What do you mean?"

"I had forgotten my phone. I came back to get it and found him talking on it."

Clay and Nathan exchanged a glance with raised brows. Clay opened the door and looked at the prisoner in the back seat. "What were you doing on her phone?"

The man glared then turned his gaze to the opposite window, jaw clamped tight.

Clay shook his head. "Right." He shut the door and locked him inside. "Guess he's not going to talk without some coercion."

"What did you do when you found him on your phone?" Nathan asked her.

"He had his back to me and I asked him what he was doing. He turned around fast and knocked a bunch of papers off the desk. He started scrambling to pick them up and I told him to stop. Some of those were tax documents that I didn't exactly want him seeing. Not that I have anything to hide," she said with a shrug, "but it wasn't his business—and he was making a bigger mess trying to help. He knocked over the can of pens and then tripped over a chair. I realize now he probably did that to cover up whatever he was doing, but at the time, I just wanted him out."

Clay nodded. "What happened after that?"

"He finally settled himself in the chair and said he'd left his phone in his car and didn't think I'd mind if he used mine. It was definitely kind of weird, but he was so nice about it and apologized so profusely that I didn't think anything else about it—or even remember the incident." She looked at the man in the back of the cruiser. "Until now."

"And then you had your accident."

"Yes. About an hour later. It took me a while to get the papers and everything cleaned up and back in order. I was Christine's only lesson that day, so she was fine with waiting on me. We finally got out to the pasture and well...you know the rest. Pete went crazy."

"You think that's a coincidence?"

She frowned. "But he wouldn't have had time to do anything to Pete. He was already saddled and waiting on me. Christine arrived and I watched Larry leave again."

Clay nodded. "It's a good thing Christine arrived when she did. Bowen might have come back and planned to get rid of you at that point."

Becca blanched. "So what stopped him the first time?"

Clay shrugged. "Who knows? Maybe he was just

checking the place out to see who was around and if he would be able to do it without getting caught."

She shivered and wrapped her arms around her middle.

Nathan slid an arm across her shoulders and brought her against his side.

"All right," Clay said. "I'll get this guy to lockup, then I'll check the time of that call against the one the dead guy, Donny Torres, received from Becca's phone. If it lines up then we might have something."

"But you said someone called that number several times," Becca said. "I only saw Mr. Bowen—or whoever he is—that once. He wouldn't have had access to my phone the other times."

"What if he's not working alone?" Nathan said.

"I was thinking that, too." Clay scrubbed a hand down his face. "I'm going to take this guy in and make sure he's nice and comfortable in his cell, then we'll do a little more digging into who he is and who he hangs out with."

"I want to be there when they question him," she said.

Clay shook his head. "You don't need to be there. You've already ID'd him as someone who'd trespassed before. We've got a name to go with him. Even if it's an alias, it's a start. We'll print him and see what turns up."

Clay climbed into the cruiser and rolled the window down. "And then I'm going to sleep for a couple of hours. Try to stay out of trouble until I can do that, okay?"

Becca rolled her eyes and Nathan crossed his arms with a scowl. "We'll do our best."

Clay waved a hand. "I'm kidding. Sort of."

He drove away with Larry Bowen staring out the

window, the look in his eyes chilling, promising retribution. Lance followed close behind.

Nathan ran a hand through his hair.

"What are you thinking?" she asked.

"I'm thinking our plan worked, but we're not out of the woods yet."

"Because he was working with someone?"

"Yes."

Becca turned to walk back into the house. A sharp crack ripped through the air and she spun, only to slam into Nathan. He clamped his arms around her, keeping his body between her and the direction that he thought the bullet had come from. "Run to the house!"

"Clay!"

"Go, Becca!"

She stopped protesting and they raced to the house together with Nathan covering her back.

Jack raced next to him to catch up with them just as Nathan threw open the door and shoved her inside. "Stay here and call for help!"

"Nathan, no—" She broke off when he turned on his heel and raced back to Clay, his prisoner and the cruiser. Lance was already on the scene, pulling Clay out of the car.

From the way the man was moving, Nathan didn't think he was hurt. Lance kept his back to Clay, who slid Larry Bowen from the vehicle and laid him on the ground.

Nathan dropped to his knees beside Bowen and looked at Clay. "You okay?"

"Yeah." He sighed. "But he's not."

"No." Nathan pressed his fingers against the man's neck, but the bullet had done its damage to Bowen's face. "He's dead. Probably didn't know what hit him."

"Great," Clay said. "Just great. I wanted him alive."

"And someone figured he was better off dead."

Clay's eyes met Nathan's. "Yeah. The same someone who thinks Becca should be, too."

Two hours later, Becca opened the refrigerator while Nathan took a seat at the kitchen table. "Want some tea?"

"Sure."

"I can't believe this." Shaking, she pulled the pitcher out and poured two glasses, the liquid sloshing over the sides.

Nathan rose, took the pitcher from her and set it on the counter. He gripped her upper arms in a gentle clasp. "You're going to be okay, Becca."

"I'm scared."

"I know you are. I'm scared for you."

She pulled away from him and handed him one of the glasses. At the table, she sat in the nearest chair while he sank back into the one opposite. "You didn't have your vest on," he said.

She rubbed her eyes. "I know. I saw Lady Lou get out of the barn and ran out of the house without thinking about it. Not that it mattered. The gun was aimed at my head, not my torso."

"True."

"That was scary."

"Terrifying."

She sighed. "You know, I don't want to believe it, but I keep coming back to my father as the one behind all of this."

"You really think he'd try to kill you?"

Tears formed and she blinked them away. "No. Of course not." She fell silent then sighed. "Then again…"

"Yeah?"

Her gaze met his. "I really don't know if he would go to such lengths to get me to quit this ranch or not. How sad is that? What kind of awful daughter am I to actually consider that my father would do something like this? To think that he would hire people like the man who was arrested today. How can I entertain such thoughts about my own father?"

"I think we need to take a trip to Nashville to see him."

She bit her lip. "Can we do that and be safe? Someone's already tried to run me over the side of the mountain. I'd be afraid they'd try again."

"I know. We'll have to work out the security details, but I think you need to talk to your parents face-to-face."

She shuddered and he scooted his chair closer to wrap an arm around her shoulders. She buried her face in his chest, and he simply held her for the next few minutes.

The knock on the door startled them both. Jack barked and got to his feet. Nathan jumped up and placed a hand on his weapon.

Becca stood, too. "I don't think the person trying to kill me is going to knock.

"Probably not, but we're not taking any chances." Nathan glanced through the screen. "It's your neighbor."

Becca stepped up behind him. "Jean, hi, come on in."

Jean walked into the house and Becca motioned for her to have a seat at the table. "Can I get you anything? Tea? Water?"

"No, no. I'm fine, thanks." She slipped into the chair on the end. "I just came over to ask you a favor."

"You should have called."

The woman shook her head. "Well, if you say yes, and I'm pretty sure you will, I'll need my truck."

"Of course. What is it?"

"Could I borrow a barrel of feed from you? I have some on order, but they haven't been delivered yet. I could run into town and get some, but I don't want to be gone too long from Hank. He's not feeling well and I hate to leave him."

Becca jumped up. "Absolutely. I have two barrels in the barn you can take tonight."

"Oh thank you, dear girl. I was hoping you'd have some to share."

Nathan was already pulling on his gloves. "I can put them in your truck." He looked at Becca. "You want me to use the two barrels at the back?"

She nodded.

"All right. You two ladies stay put. I'll be back."

He left and Jean leaned forward. "I've been so wrapped up in what's going on over at my ranch that I haven't checked in on you like I should have. How are you holding up?"

"I'm holding—and healing. It's taking time, of course, and I'm not the most patient person around, but I'm getting there." Should she mention the incident with Larry Bowen or not? "Thank you very much for your help with the lessons. I hate that we took you away from Hank. I didn't realize that he was sick."

"It's just a nasty cold, but I'm watching him close to make sure it doesn't develop into pneumonia like it did a couple of years ago."

The woman was in her late sixties, petite and energetic. Becca had immediately liked her engaging personality and infectious laughter. "I hear you're still having trouble over here."

Becca drew in a breath and nodded as she let it out slowly. "I am."

"Sorry about that. Is there anything I can do to help?"

"No. But you might want to steer clear of my place until the trouble is over. I'm not very healthy to be around."

Jean waved a hand. "I'm not too worried."

She didn't understand the gravity of the situation. Most likely she wouldn't need to. She'd get her feed and head back to her ranch to take care of her animals and her husband and that would be that.

The door opened and Nathan stepped back inside. "Got you all loaded up. You're good to go."

Jean stood and so did Becca. "Thank you so much," the woman said. "This is a huge help."

"No problem."

"Are you going to be able to unload those barrels?" Nathan asked.

"I've got a couple of helpers that come over for a few hours each day. We'll get them where they need to be. And when my shipment comes in, I'll have them bring your replacement feed."

"No problem."

Jean drove away and Nathan returned to the table. "So. When's a good time to go to Nashville?"

Becca rubbed her forehead. "I don't even know." She glanced at the clock. "I haven't talked to my parents in months—like close to a year." She paused. "I could probably track down someone my father works with and ask."

"Your dad's a doctor, right?"

"A surgeon."

"Right."

"And my mother is a lawyer."

He blinked. "Yes, seems like I knew that. The Wrangler's Corner power couple."

"Hmm. Until Dad took the job as chief of surgery at St. Thomas in Nashville."

"And then moved you away from me." He smiled. "Why don't you make that call?"

Her parents had let her finish her junior year of high school before whisking her away to Nashville. She'd been devastated to leave Wrangler's Corner. Which was probably why she found her way back here. She reached for her phone. And realized she didn't have it. With a sigh, she rose and walked to the counter and retrieved the device. "I've got to learn to keep this on me."

"As long as it's in reaching distance."

She dialed her father's number. Of course it went to voice mail. She hung up and dialed the hospital emergency department number. "This is Becca Price. Could I speak to Rachel Goodman?"

"Price? Any relation to Dr. George Price?"

"His daughter." She'd admit it if it got Rachel on the phone.

"Wow. Okay. And you want to speak to Dr. Goodman?"

"Yes, please."

"Just a minute. Let me see if I can track her down for you."

Rachel always knew where her father was. She was one of his surgeons who had her eye on his job whenever he was ready to retire. He was only fifty-two so she didn't think that was going to happen for a while. He liked his position of power too much—doing what he did best. Controlling lives, feeling like he was cheating death because without him and his scalpel, his patient would have died. And while that might be true, she believed God had more control over that part than her father did. He didn't see it that way, though.

"Hello?"

"Hi, Rachel, this is Becca."

"Becca? I haven't heard from you in forever. How are you?" The words were pleasant enough, but she could hear the chaos in the background and knew the woman needed to get going.

"I'm fine, thanks. Listen, I won't keep you, but you're my only hope for tracking down my father. To make a long story short, he's not taking my phone calls." No need to go into details. "Do you know if he's going to be around today and in his office? What time would be good to drop in on him?"

"Hold on a second and let me check the surgery schedule." There was a short pause before she came back on. "It looks like he's going to be in his office between four and five this afternoon."

"That will work," Becca said. "Thanks so much."

"Do you want me to tell him that you are going to come see him?"

"No!" Becca realized she'd nearly shouted the word. She softened her tone. "No, that's okay. I want to surprise him." There was no way her father had shared with Rachel the grief his stubborn daughter was causing him, so there was no reason for Rachel to suspect that the surprise wouldn't be a good one.

"He's not a big fan of surprises or people just dropping in on him. Are you sure you want to do that?"

Okay, maybe the woman knew Becca's father better than she thought.

"I'm sure."

"Becca, he'll kill me if I don't tell him you're coming by."

"He'll be fine, Rachel. Don't say anything, please. He won't even have to know we talked."

"He'll know." The woman sighed. "Fine. I won't say anything. It's not my business to get involved in family matters."

"Thank you."

"Well, stop by and say hello if you get a chance."

"I will."

Becca hung up and blew out a breath.

"Well?" Nathan asked.

"I think we're good to go. I can't believe I'm actually going to do this, but I'm ready when you are."

"I'm going to call Clay and see if he can set up an escort for us."

She nodded. "Okay…"

His eyes lingered on hers. "What?" he asked.

"What did you mean that my parents moved me away from you?"

"They did. At least, I took it personally. It was one of the saddest days of my life when you told me you were moving."

"It wasn't exactly the best day of my life, either." She paused.

"You knew I had a huge crush on you, didn't you?"

Her jaw dropped. "What?"

He lifted a brow. "You seriously didn't know?"

"No, you never did anything about it."

A short laugh escaped him. "I didn't dare. I cherished your friendship too much."

"But you were the popular basketball star in all the honors classes. You could have had any girl in the school. They fell all over themselves to get you to notice them."

He didn't smile. "But not you."

She flushed. The heat traveled from the base of her throat and into her cheeks. "No, I didn't know how to flirt and be all prissy like those girls. As much as I wanted to, it just wasn't me. So, I didn't."

"And you noticed who I wanted to hang out with."

True. But it didn't stop him from going out with the other girls. Occasionally. And never one for very long.

He gave another low laugh. "And as for the honors classes, you were in those, too. I was a sixteen-year-old kid without a dollar to my name. You were the rich kid who lived in the big ranch on the hill with a maid and all the boys chasing after you."

Becca swallowed. "I didn't care about all that. The boys or the house. The boys were just interested in my parents' money, and the only thing I loved about that house was the horses. I spent most of my days riding and working in the barn."

"I know. You were really focused on that. And besides, you spent every weekend at competitions. You didn't have time for a boyfriend. Even I could see that."

"True. Maybe." She glanced at him out of the corner of her eye. "But it might have been nice to have the option."

"You mean you would have given me the time of day? Other than hanging out as a friend, I mean?" He scoffed. "Come on."

She shrugged. "You never know."

"And I guess we won't now, will we?"

"No. I guess not." She looked away, then turned back to him. "Why did you kiss me? Was it to satisfy some kind of leftover teenage crush curiosity?"

He held her gaze and then shook his head. "No. I wasn't even thinking about that."

"Then what?"

"I was thinking about how strong you are. How determined and honorable…and how much I admire you."

"You admire me?" She frowned. "I don't know that I deserve your admiration. Some days I feel like a huge failure."

"Becca, surely you can see how amazing you are. Not everyone could have accomplished so much in such a short time."

"Maybe. I mean, yes, I know I've accomplished a lot. It takes hard work and determination to get through medical school and I won't make light of that. But I'm really not so sure about the strong part. Some days I don't feel very strong."

He gripped her fingers and the sleeping butterflies in her belly fluttered to life. "I don't think you give yourself enough credit."

"Maybe not."

"You're a doctor."

"I am. On paper anyway. And in practice, for a while."

"And yet you gave it all up to chase your dreams."

"Hmm. I wouldn't say I gave it all up."

"What would you say then?"

She blew out a low breath. "I would say that I put a career that I love on hold to see if I could do this. To find out if I can have a successful barn, watch children's eyes light up when they ride a horse for the first time, watch a student get the form right for a jump. All of that. It's so amazing. Almost as amazing as surgery. Sometimes more so." She paused. "Depends on the surgery."

"Exactly. Admirable."

She bit her lip and he leaned in. Her heart thundered in her ears as she realized he was going to kiss her again.

TWELVE

Her lips beckoned him. His deception stopped him. What was he doing? He couldn't keep kissing her, confusing her until he came clean. He sat back with a mental slap upside his head. A romance with her wasn't an option until she knew everything.

She blinked. "What is it?"

"I… Look, there are some things we should probably talk about."

"What?"

"My reason for being here, for one."

Now it was her turn to frown. "You're here to help me on the ranch, right?"

"Well, yes…"

"Then what are you talking about?"

Would she send him away? Would she hate him forever? Would she leave herself open and vulnerable to whoever wanted her dead? Once again those thoughts stilled his tongue.

"I—"

The knock on the door sent waves of relief through him. He needed to keep his mouth shut. "I'll get it."

He turned to see Brody Mac standing on the front

porch. Nathan opened the door and stepped back. Brody Mac walked inside and pulled his hat off. "Hi, Becca."

"Hi, Brody Mac. I'm glad to see you back here. Is everything all right at home?"

"Yes. I think so. My daddy left, so my mama is singing again. She only sings when she's happy."

"I see."

"I just came to tell you that I'm going on an overnight field trip with my class so I won't be here tomorrow."

Becca nodded. "Thanks for letting me know."

He shuffled his feet. "Did Nathan help you out?"

"What?"

"The other day. I saw him in your office. He said he was doing something to help you. I like that, Becca. I want you to have all the help you need because I like you. I can help you more if you need me to. You just have to tell me, okay?"

Becca gave a slow nod, her brow furrowed, and Nathan's heart dropped into his boots. He cleared his throat. "I'm going to give Clay a call and see if we can get an escort to Nashville."

"Okay." He could feel her eyes following him as he stepped into the den. He dialed Clay's number.

"Hello?"

"We've got a problem."

"We sure do."

Nathan frowned. "What's going on?"

"Larry Bowen had nothing on him to tell us if he was working with someone else or not, at least nothing that would help us ID someone, but he had ten thousand in cash."

"Whoa."

He lifted his eyes to the blank spot where Becca said she wanted to hang his stocking. His heart ached, his deception killing him. She trusted him, had invited him into her home and her life—maybe even her heart? And here he was, lying to her.

"Nathan? You there?"

Nathan blinked and focused back on Clay. "I'm here. So, you think that money was for taking out Becca?"

"There's not a doubt in my mind." The stone-cold fury in Clay's voice echoed the rising emotion in his own chest.

"Clay, maybe we can take this in a different direction," Nathan said. "Time to go on the defensive."

"What are you talking about?"

Nathan explained their idea about confronting Becca's father.

Clay sighed. "I'm not sure that's a good idea. I really don't have the manpower, especially with Trent still in the hospital. With Bowen's death, I've called for help on the state level. Investigators should be arriving within the hour."

"Good, you'll need them."

"Exactly. Which means that right now I have two open deputy positions to fill and only three deputies to cover the entire town of Wrangler's Corner. I'm sorry, Nathan, I can't help you out on this. At least not today."

Nathan pursed his lips. "It's okay, I understand."

"But…"

"But what?"

"Give me a few minutes to think on it."

"Fine. You think, but don't hang up yet."

"What else is going on?" Nathan sympathized with the weariness in the man's voice.

He walked to the kitchen and saw Becca wiping down the countertops. Nathan returned to the den. "Brody Mac spilled the beans about me being in Becca's office the other day. She's going to ask me about it and I'm going to have to tell her the truth. I won't lie to her." Not anymore.

"I know. Just try to delay answering if you can. Can you distract her?"

"Distract Becca? That's a good one."

"Right." Clay sighed. "Do what you have to do on that score. Let me see what I can do with getting you an escort to Nashville. Talk to you shortly."

Nathan hung up and closed his eyes. Now might not be a bad time to pray. He walked into the kitchen. "Clay's working on getting us some protection to get to Nashville."

"Good." She turned and opened her mouth.

His phone buzzed. "Hold on. It's Clay calling back." He lifted the device to his ear, grateful for the timely interruption. "Hey."

"All right. Since the state people are going to be here shortly, Lance is going to follow you to Nashville. What time do you want to leave?"

Lance Goode. Amber's husband. "As soon as he can get here."

Becca wasn't sure what to pray. On the one hand, she wanted to know who was trying to kill her. On the other, she certainly didn't want it to be her own father. Anxiety twisted inside her. She was glad Lance was driving. He'd decided they should take the cruiser to make a statement to anyone who might have the idea to cause them trouble.

Nathan sat in the front seat and she almost wished she'd asked him to sit in the back next to her. It would have made it easier to hold his hand.

But no. Sitting in the back was good. It would give

her time to think and not be distracted by Nathan and the fact that she was attracted to him.

Unfortunately, he wasn't in Wrangler's Corner for the long haul and she was. At some point, he'd return to Nashville and to the job he'd left to heal.

Brody Mac's words came back to her. What had Nathan been doing in her office? She wanted to know but didn't want to bring it up in front of Lance.

Knowing she could blow the whole surprise thing if her mother decided to tell her father, Becca decided it was worth taking a chance on. She shot a text to her, stating where she would be and at what time. Becca didn't mention seeing her father, just that she would be at the hospital. Sadness engulfed her. She wanted to see her mother. To hug her and talk with her. But as long as her father demanded her mother not speak to her, she wouldn't. For someone who could rule the courtroom with strength and passion, she was a complete wimp when it came to standing up to her control-freak husband.

"You okay?"

Becca glanced up to see Nathan looking back at her. She nodded and swiped the stray tear that had escaped. She cleared her throat. "I'll be okay. I just want this over with."

"Yeah."

What was she going to say? *Hi, Dad. Did you hire someone to kill me?* Oh yes, that would go over well. She grimaced.

"Becca?"

She raised a brow.

"Don't stress over it."

"Don't stress over it?" She laughed. "I wish I could take that advice."

She fell silent, going back to her mental rehearsal of what she was going to say to her father when she saw him for the first time in a year. The day she'd closed on the ranch, he'd showed up at the bank to let her know she was no longer a part of his family, no longer welcome in his home. As far as he was concerned, she no longer existed.

She'd only admitted to herself and her counselor in Nashville that she'd nearly caved. Had been very tempted to fall into her childhood and teen pattern of following his commands. But Lisa's words rang in her ears from one of their earlier counseling sessions. "Only you can decide for you what you truly want. Whether it's using that medical degree you worked so hard for or branching out and trying something new, it's something only you can decide with God's direction. You control your future, not your father."

And the truth was, she'd prayed about it but had never gotten a clear sense of whether or not it was the right thing to do. So, she'd gone with it. Resigned from her position at the hospital, bought the ranch in Wrangler's Corner, and now look where she was. Had it all been a huge mistake? From where she sat now, it certainly looked like it.

She blinked when Lance turned into the parking lot of the hospital. Time had passed quickly between her thoughts and her vigilant mirror watching.

Lance pulled the vehicle into the police parking spot by the entrance to the emergency department. She'd chosen this entrance because the nearest elevator went straight to the second floor. Which was where she would find her father.

Her knees shook and she clenched her fingers into fists to stop the fine tremor.

"Becca?" Nathan's soft voice jerked her from her thoughts. "You okay?"

"Yes. No. I don't know."

"Now you sound like me."

She flicked a glance at Lance who stood at the door, waiting. "I'm just nervous. Do you know what it took for me to stand up to my father—my parents—and walk out of the house after I told them what I planned to do?"

She'd been living with them and saving money. It had worked out well. They had a guesthouse separate from the main house, and she'd been very comfortable there. They also had the barn and the horses that she often worked with on her days off.

But it wasn't enough. She wanted her own place, her own horses. And they simply didn't understand that.

"I imagine it was pretty tough."

"That's one way to put it. I was so scared of how they were going to react that I went ahead and packed my car just in case."

"And?"

"It was a good thing I did."

"Wow."

"Yeah." When her father had ordered her from the house, she'd simply walked out, climbed into her Lexus and driven away.

She'd cried all the way to Wrangler's Corner, but she'd closed on the ranch the week before and it was time to get busy working it to get it ready for business. She'd sold her Lexus and bought a truck that was much more suitable for ranch living.

And now she'd come full circle.

"You don't have to go in there," she said. "I can ask him myself."

"No." He raised a brow and she shook her head. "Let's get this over with."

"You're sure?"

"I'm sure."

His hand closed around hers as she stepped from the car. She was very glad he was with her.

She led the way inside the building, her steps sure even while her heart beat like a wild bird trapped in a cage. She'd never been good at confrontation and truly, had she not done the counseling with Lisa, she wouldn't be doing this. But, she'd finally come to the conclusion that her relationship with her parents was worth fighting for—but only if her father wasn't trying to have her killed.

She found his office, her feet automatically walking a route she'd taken many times. The door stood open. She drew in a breath and felt Nathan's hand at the small of her back. His strength bolstered her own.

She stepped forward and rapped her knuckles on the open door. The man at the desk looked up and she faced her father for the first time in a year. She didn't bother trying to smile at him. "Hi, Dad."

THIRTEEN

The man actually flinched. Nathan blinked. Dr. Price had aged over the years and not particularly well. He had a full head of gray hair, and his blue eyes had bags that indicated he was either working too hard or wasn't sleeping well at night.

Probably both.

Nathan stayed just outside the door so he could listen and intervene if necessary. Lance stood at the end of the hall, keeping watch on those who passed by.

"Becca."

He had a pleasant voice, a low bass that sounded like it could soothe a scared patient—or intimidate a rebellious daughter. Nathan couldn't tell which way the conversation might go from that one word.

"I need to talk to you," Becca said.

"Have you come to your senses and sold your ranch?"

"No, sir, and I don't plan on it any time soon."

"Then we have nothing to talk about. Shut the door as you leave."

He looked down at his laptop and Becca's back wilted at the harsh words. Nathan took a step forward, ready to blast the man. Becca looked back at him, the hurt in her eyes nearly his undoing. Then she shook her head and straightened her spine. "I'm not leaving yet." She took two more steps then slid into the chair facing her father's desk. "I have a question for you. Once you answer it to my satisfaction, I'll be happy to leave."

He glanced up and met Nathan's gaze. Dr. Price's eyes narrowed then dismissed him. The man huffed. "What is it?"

"Are you trying to kill me? And I mean that in the literal sense. Do you hate me so much," her voice quivered and she cleared her throat, "that you would rather see me dead than working the ranch?"

The silence nearly deafened him and Nathan's tension rose with each passing second.

Becca's father finally drew in a breath and rubbed a hand down the side of his face. He shook his head and squinted at her like he'd never seen her before. "I'm sorry, what did you ask me?"

Becca lifted her chin. "You heard me."

Leaning back and crossing his arms, he seemed to search for words even as he searched his daughter's face. Nathan almost felt sorry for him.

Finally, he leaned forward.

"Well, that's one way to get my attention. Why would you ask me such a thing?"

"Because someone's trying to either kill me or run me off the ranch, and the only person with motive that I could think of was you."

More silence.

Nathan wasn't sure if that was a good thing or not.

"What exactly has happened that you felt you had to come ask me that?"

Becca told him about the incidents. The attack in the barn, the shootings and being run off the road. The more she talked, the more the man's face paled. Nathan didn't relax, but his anxiety eased. For all his arrogance and bluster, Dr. Price loved his daughter. At least it looked like he did. Could he be that good of an actor?

Nathan's tension returned as another thought occurred. Or was the man simply shocked she'd figured it out?

The doctor rose from his seat and paced to the window. "I don't know what to say, Becca."

"Just answer the question and I'll leave."

He turned back to face her and spread his hands. "I simply don't know what to say."

"You said that already."

Clasping his hands behind his back, he clicked his heels together and raised his gaze to lock it on hers. "I really have to say the words?"

"Yes, Dad, I believe you do."

"No, Rebecca," he said, "I'm not trying to kill you, and I didn't hire anyone to carry out those things that you just described."

Becca sat stone-still for a brief moment before she gave a short nod and stood. "All right. Thank you for answering me."

Her father continued to stare at her. "You don't believe me."

Frankly, Nathan wasn't sure he did either, but he was leaning toward the idea that the man had had nothing to do with any of it and was blown away that Becca had actually asked him if he was involved somehow.

Becca hesitated then sighed. "I don't know what to believe, to be honest."

Another flinch from the usually rock-steady man. He drew in a deep breath and Nathan thought he saw a sheen of tears before it disappeared. "I might be furious with you for throwing your career away, but I'd never hurt you."

She didn't speak for a moment. Then said, "As someone once said, there are all kinds of hurt. Thank you for seeing me." She turned on her heel and walked out of his office. In the hallway, Nathan took her hand. She stopped and closed her eyes for a moment.

"What is it?"

"I can't leave like this."

Her father seemed shocked that she would believe that he had something to do with the attempts on her life, but to Becca, the conclusion wasn't all that far-fetched.

Of course she didn't want to believe it, but…she drew in a fortifying breath and walked back into his office. He hadn't moved from his spot by the window. "Dad, I love you. We haven't always seen eye to eye on everything, and yes, that's an understatement. But I love you. I'm sorry if I hurt you by asking, but I—" She rubbed a hand over her eyes and pinched the bridge of her nose. A headache had started as soon as she'd stepped into the hospital. Now the nausea was getting ready to kick in. She had to get out of here. "Anyway, I have to go. Please tell Mom I love her, too."

There, she'd done all she could do. The ball was in his court, so to speak.

He said nothing, simply turned from the window to stare at her, a strange look in his blue eyes.

She sighed and once again left his office. This time she kept walking, Nathan at her side. "You did good," he said in a low voice. "As much as that hurt you—and I think him as well—it was the right thing to do."

"I'm glad you're so confident in that."

"I'm confident in you."

She stopped walking and turned to look up at him. Tears wanted to fall, but she held them back. "Thank you for that. I think with everything going on, I've lost some of my confidence, my faith that I can do anything I set my mind to." Sad, her heart heavy, she headed for the exit, desperately glad Nathan was at her side.

"Becca?"

Becca's heart thudded. She stumbled and only Nathan's hand on her upper arm kept her from falling to the tile floor. She looked to her left. "Mom?"

"Oh, Becca. I've missed you so."

Becca didn't hesitate. She ran into her mother's outstretched arms and buried her face into her shoulder, inhaling her familiar scent. A hint of vanilla and spice. "I've missed you, too."

"I couldn't stay away when you said you'd be here."

Becca pulled back and searched the woman's beloved eyes. "But you can't return my phone call?"

Her mother frowned. "What call?"

"I called and left you a message."

"I didn't get it." She pulled her phone from the side pocket of her purse and tapped the screen. She shook her head. "There. See? Nothing."

Becca looked and sure enough, there was nothing to indicate she'd called. "I know I had the right number, I left a message on your voice mail."

"I don't know. I would have called you back had I seen it."

"Really?"

Tears flooded her mother's eyes once more. "Really. This distance is so foolish. I've been praying for a year that your father would see reason, but he doesn't seem to be any closer now than the day you left."

"If you felt that way, why wouldn't you talk to me? Discounting my most recent attempt, I called you every day for three months."

"I know." She sighed. "In the beginning, your father demanded I not answer. He said our refusal to talk to you would bring you back around. He said we had to stick to what we said."

Which was they were done with her until she saw reason. Their interpretation of reason anyway. "I see."

"But I'm done with that. Now that I've seen you again, I can't go back to the way things were."

"Even if Dad refuses to change his position?"

"Even if." She squeezed Becca's hand and looked past her. "Now, who is this young man who's been watching us with eagle eyes?"

Becca turned. "Oh, you remember Nathan Williams, don't you?"

"Nathan? Of course! You and Becca were such good friends before we moved. She was so sad to leave you behind."

"Good to see you again, Mrs. Price. And I missed her, too. It's been good to reconnect. I just wish it was under better circumstances."

Her mother frowned, her flawlessly plucked brows drawing together at the bridge of her nose. "What do you mean?"

"It's a long story," Becca said. "Do you have time to go down to the cafeteria for some food? I'm starving." Becca wanted to get her mother's perspective on the whole thing. She hadn't planned to tell her anything, but she wasn't 100 percent sure her father would fill her in.

"Yes. Just let me call the office and let them know I'm taking the rest of the day off."

Becca gaped. Her mother never took time off. Ever.

A slow peace started to fill her. And it was really nice to see God answering a prayer right before her eyes. Maybe things would be okay after all.

If they could just catch the person trying to kill her.

It didn't take as long to recount everything as Nathan had thought it might. Lance stayed in the background, eating a sandwich and keeping an eye on their surroundings. Becca talked while they ate. When she finished the story her mother gaped, horror in her eyes. "Oh my, Becca, are you serious? Someone is trying to kill you?"

"It sure seems that way."

Her mother pressed a hand over her heart. "I don't even know what to say."

"I don't, either."

"And you actually asked your father if he'd hired someone to do so?"

Becca's face reddened. "I know. I'm a horrible daughter."

"No. Not at all. It's amazing to me."

She blinked. "What?"

"That you're not letting him bully you. That once you made your decision to take charge of your life, you did. And you haven't looked back. I admire that. I'm proud of you." She drew in a deep breath. "And I guess it's up to me to learn from you."

"What do you mean?"

"I mean it's time for me to grow a spine. I'm not letting him dictate my relationship with you. Not anymore." She reached for Becca's hand. "Oh, honey, the fact that someone is trying to kill you scares me to death—but it's not your father."

"How do you know?"

Mrs. Price's mouth opened, then closed. She sighed.

"Come on, Becca. You know he wouldn't do something like that."

Becca bit her lip and looked away. Nathan wanted desperately to intervene but forced himself to stay still and keep his mouth shut. He seemed to be doing a lot of that around her lately.

"You really think he would hire someone to kill you?" Mrs. Price said. The whisper was low, but Nathan heard it.

Becca pressed her fingers to her eyes before looking at her mother. "I don't want to believe it, of course. With everything in me, I don't. I just…don't know what to believe anymore."

Her mother sighed. "Go home. I'll get to the bottom of this." She looked at Nathan. "Is someone going to be with her? To make sure she's protected?"

"At all times."

"All right, then. And when you catch him, I want to prosecute." She reached for Becca once more and they hugged. Becca seemed loath to let her go but finally did.

Her mother cupped her face. "I don't know why I didn't get your call. I suspect your father saw it come in and deleted it. But I'll be sure to keep my phone with me at all times from now on. If you need me, call me. In the meantime, I'll call you after I manage to get your father alone and have an uninterrupted conversation with him."

"All right."

One more hug and Mrs. Price turned on her heel and strode to the elevator that would take her to her husband's office. Nathan wished he could be a fly on the wall. Becca didn't move until her mother was no longer in sight and then let out a sigh. "I'm not sure that did any good with my father, but I can't tell you the peace

and joy I feel at this reconciliation with my mother."
He wrapped an arm around her shoulder, and his heart
thudded a bit faster when she snuggled up next to him.
"Thank you for being here with me."

He nodded. "I wouldn't want to be anywhere else."
He blew out a low breath. He was going to have to come
clean with her. And soon. His jaw tightened. He'd tell
her everything on the ride back to the ranch. Then beg
her not to make him leave. If she was determined to
send him away, he'd just camp out on her property. And
if she didn't want him there, what was she going to do
about it? Call Clay? Clay would be his backup.

He gave her shoulders another squeeze. "Come on.
Let's get out of here." He waved to Lance who'd been
waiting quietly, watching the people and the doors.
Lance nodded that he was right behind them.

On the way back to the car, several people stopped
Becca and asked her when she was coming back. She
simply smiled and shrugged. "I'm happy doing what
I'm doing right now. We'll see."

When they were almost to the exit, Becca stopped
and laid a hand on his arm. "Wait, I need to get something from the gift shop."

"What?"

"Something I just saw in the window. Hang out here
for a minute, okay?"

Mystified, but willing to wait, Nathan nodded then
stopped her. "Stay here with Lance and let me take a
quick look."

"Why?"

"Because. Just hold on."

Nathan walked inside the store and wrinkled his
nose at the strong smell from the scented candles. But
one glance around and he had his answer. Chock-full

of Christmas decorations, flowers and other odds and ends, it had only one way in and one way out. He exited and nodded to Becca. "Want me to go back in with you?"

"Nope. I want you to stay right here." She gave him a quick, mysterious smile before disappearing into the shop.

"What's she doing?" Lance asked.

Nathan shrugged. "Beats me. She said she needed to get something."

"What's the layout?"

"It's small, overcrowded with inventory, and needs some serious ventilation, but the only other person in there is the cashier. She's fine."

Lance fell back a little and Nathan waited. He didn't have to wait long. Soon, she came out holding a brown paper bag. "I'm ready now."

"What did you get?"

"Just a little something I decided I wanted. I'll share it with you later."

"Chocolate?"

She smiled. "It's a secret."

"It's got to be chocolate."

"Stop. I'm not telling. Now let's go."

Nathan decided to let her keep her little secret, and together the three of them walked to the front door of the hospital. "Stay here," Lance said. "I'll get the car and bring it around. No sense in walking out in the open for the time it would take."

Nathan nodded and wrapped an arm around her shoulder. "We'll be watching for you."

His eyes scanned the circle that served as the drop-off and pick-up point for the hospital. It looked clear, but he couldn't help wonder if they shouldn't use a different entrance. "Pick us up at the emergency department," he said.

Lance lifted a brow and nodded. "Good idea." He walked out the door and Nathan tilted his head toward the other end of the hospital. "Let's take a walk."

She drew in a deep breath and let it out slowly. "Right. Let's do that."

Finally, they were seated in his vehicle. Lance in the front seat and, to her surprise, Nathan climbed into the back with her. "We'll let you chauffer this one," he told Lance. Lance grinned at him in the rearview mirror and Nathan ignored the look. He wanted to sit with her. Lance's phone rang. "Hang on a second." He got out of the cruiser and took the call.

Becca raised a brow at Nathan. "You okay?" she asked.

"Yes, just conflicted about something."

"What's that?"

Nathan shook his head. "Just a decision I need to make."

She frowned. "Okay."

He squeezed her fingers. "Don't worry about it. I'll figure it out."

"I'm a pretty good listener."

"I know. We'll talk later. I don't need Lance as an audience." He smiled and changed the subject. "Sounds like your Christmas might be brighter than you thought."

"I certainly hope so." She paused and tucked the paper back under her thigh and fastened her seat belt. "And if you don't want to talk about whatever is bothering you, tell me something else."

"What's that?"

"What did Brody Mac mean when he said you were

in my office helping me? What were you doing in my office?"

She hadn't forgotten about that one. Nathan blinked and then shrugged. "I was checking to see if you had a landline." It was the truth. Not the whole truth, but at least it wasn't an outright lie.

"For what?"

"To see if there was some way to put a security system out there. At least on the house."

"Oh." She shook her head. "I don't have one and I can't afford a security system right now."

"You might have to find a way to afford one."

"I have Jack."

"Jack likes everyone. He's not the most reliable watchdog."

She grimaced and he knew she couldn't argue the point. She fell silent and leaned her head against the window. Nathan would let her rest instead of shoving a stick in the hornet's nest. He might be taking the coward's way out, but he'd forgotten Lance would be within hearing range on the drive home and decided he could wait to tell her about his deception.

For now.

FOURTEEN

When Lance turned into the drive, Becca noted Zeb's truck there. "That's odd," she said.

Nathan frowned. "What?"

"I wasn't expecting him to be here."

The vet came out of the barn and Jack bounded beside him. Zeb pulled up short when he spotted the police cruiser, then removed his gloves and shoved them into his coat pockets. Nathan stepped out of the driver's side and Becca slipped out of the passenger seat. She shut the door behind her. "Everything okay?"

"Yeah, Brody Mac called and said one of the horses was acting funny. I didn't know you'd be back so soon or I would have just called you to let you know."

"He called you instead of me?"

Zeb shrugged. "I'm the vet. I guess he figured I'd know what to do."

Becca laughed. "I guess so. Which horse?"

"Pete."

"Again?"

Zeb shrugged. "I couldn't find anything wrong with him. The abscess is healed. Everything looks good."

"Wonder what Brody Mac saw? He knows horses."

Zeb waved a hand. "I wouldn't worry about it too

much. Could be Pete's just finally feeling better and he's acting a bit frisky. I put some more ointment on his foot just in case, but it seems pretty well healed to me."

"All right, if you say so."

"I say so."

"Where's Brody Mac now?"

"He left. Drove off on the moped."

"What? Why?" She had work he could do.

"Because he said he wasn't feeling well. I checked his temperature and he was burning up with fever."

"Oh no!"

"Yeah. Hope you don't catch it."

"Okay, thanks, Zeb."

"No problem. Now I'm heading over to the Staffords. Jean's got a foal that's ready to meet the world."

"Tell her I said hello."

"Will do." He climbed into his truck and left.

She shook her head and headed for the barn with Nathan. She checked on Pete and noted the ointment residue on his hoof. The abscess looked healed to her, too. And Pete seemed to be just fine. She rubbed his nose and he nudged her hand, nibbling, looking for a treat. "I'll have to get you one in a minute, big boy." She frowned. "I sure hope Brody Mac feels better fast. It's awful to be sick like that. I may need to take a look at him. His mother won't always get him to a doctor."

"You think he'll go home?" Nathan asked.

"As long as his dad isn't there."

"Does he have a cell phone?"

"Yes."

"Let's call and verify that he's all right. I'm concerned."

She pulled her purse off her shoulder and dug through it, locating the device at the bottom. She dialed Brody

Mac's number and it went to his voice mail. "Call me when you get this, Brody Mac, okay?"

She hung up and shoved the phone in her pocket where she'd have it within easy reach. "I think I'll ride out to his house to check on him."

"Then I'm going with you."

"It's just about a mile away."

"Yep. I know where it is."

"All right, then. Since my truck is still in the shop, you can drive."

"Happy to."

She followed him to his truck and climbed in. He slipped into the driver's seat and twisted the key.

Nothing happened.

"What?" he said. "That's weird."

He popped the hood and then got out and rounded the truck. She opened the door and walked over to stand beside him.

"I think it's the battery," he said. "Dead as a doornail."

"Oh, no. Okay, well, I really want to check on Brody Mac. What do you think about riding the horses over? I could ride Pete over and you can take Lady Lou?"

He frowned. "I don't think that's a good idea. You'll be exposed."

"Not if we take the back way through the woods. It's probably safer than getting back on the road anyway."

"The back way?"

"We just cut behind the barn and head into the trees. There's a path that leads straight to the MacDougal place. We'll be exposed for a short time once we leave the barn and hit the small pasture behind it, but only for a few seconds if we gallop the horses. Once we're in the trees we're cut off from view until we get to Brody Mac's house."

He thought about it for a minute and then nodded. "That works for me."

Within minutes they had the horses saddled, and Becca sighed with relief that the process didn't seem to bother her back much. It pulled slightly, but there were no sharp pains. Maybe she was finally healing.

Becca swung into the saddle and felt the world settle into place. Whenever she was on the back of a horse, her troubles simply melted away and peace surrounded her in spite of the danger she knew they were still in. Which is why they would be careful.

The wind whipped her hair around her face and she dug the knit hat out of the pocket of her coat.

Gloves followed and she was ready. She noticed Nathan had done the same. "It's colder today."

"I know, but it's good to be in the saddle."

"I'll agree to that."

She clicked to Pete while giving him a gentle squeeze with her legs. He responded without hesitation, and they headed off into the tree line.

She was almost surprised no one shot at them in the four seconds it took them to dash into the cover of the trees.

Once there, Becca pulled on the reins and slowed Pete to a gentle walk. He walked the path that had been worn by generations before. Created to make a way from one neighbor's house to the other.

An object blocking the path just ahead caught her attention. "What's that?"

Nathan narrowed his eyes. "Stay here."

He didn't give her a chance to answer and took off ahead of her. Becca slid the rifle from the scabbard and held it across her lap. As she got closer, she could see that the object was actually a person.

Nathan swung out of the saddle and landed on the ground beside the figure then looked back at her. "It's Brody Mac!"

Becca gasped and hurried forward, stopping Pete next to Lady Lou. Carefully, so as not to move her back too fast, Becca lowered herself to the ground then quickly stepped to Brody Mac's side. "What happened?"

"He's breathing fine and he's got a good pulse, but he's got a pretty nasty head wound." Nathan pointed to the gash on the side of the man's head. "The moped is in the trees over there. I'm going to call 911." He pulled his phone from his pocket and called it in.

Becca didn't bother to spare a glance at the machine—she was too worried about her friend. Even though Nathan had some basic first aid training, Becca went ahead and checked his breathing and pulse, only to concur with Nathan's assessment.

She moved on to the rest of his body, moving him carefully, looking for broken bones or any other wounds. "The right sleeve of his coat is torn near the elbow, but he doesn't appear to be hurt. The thick material probably protected him. And there's nothing broken." She continued her assessment and came back to his head. "Can you get the first aid kit out of my saddlebag?"

"Sure." Nathan moved fast and soon she was cleaning the wound. "It's going to need some stitches. I can't get it to stop bleeding with these limited supplies. I'm just going to butterfly the edges together and hope the bandages stick long enough to get him transported to the hospital." In quick order, she had the gash shut and bandaged. "I wonder what made him crash," she said.

Nathan looked up. "I think it was a bullet."

She hesitated on a fraction of second then went back to Brody Mac's head. "What makes you think that?"

"There's no indication that he struck the ground with his head. He fell off the moped and then the bike fell over, too, but skidded into the trees. Whatever hit him had to have some serious force behind it to make that happen."

"The gash is consistent with a bullet graze." Tears tried to cloud her vision and she quickly brushed them away and refused to let them fall. "This is my fault. I should have found a way to keep him occupied somewhere else. I should have—"

"Stop. This isn't your fault."

He tilted his head at the same time she heard the sirens in the distance. "They know how to find us?"

"Yes."

Thirty minutes later, an unconscious Brody Mac was loaded on the stretcher and carried out of the woods. She and Nathan followed, leading the horses.

Once they broke through the tree line, she could see the ambulance had driven around to the back of the barn and was waiting. Becca hurried after the paramedics. "He probably has a concussion and you'll need to monitor—"

Nathan's hand on her arm stopped her. "They know what they're doing," he said softly.

She nodded and swallowed more tears. "I know. We need to let his mother know."

"What's her number? I'll call her."

Becca gave it to him and then took Pete's reins and headed for the barn. Nathan followed at a slower pace. Lady Lou plodded along behind him, completely unfazed by the events of the day.

"Yes, ma'am," Nathan said, "he's unconscious, but

should be okay when he wakes up. Other than a raging headache and a possible concussion. Do you have a way to get to the hospital? Uh-huh. Okay. Call me back if you need to."

He hung up as Becca stepped inside the barn and drew in a deep breath. She let it out slowly, trying to steady her nerves and gather her thoughts. She ran a hand over Pete's nose and he tried to nibble her fingers. "I guess I'll get the horses taken care of then."

"I'll help you."

Together, they worked in silence for the next few minutes. Becca was glad to have him in the barn with her.

Two more trips to the feed room and she should be finished. She rounded the corner into the room and leaned over to scoop the food into the bucket. Her back twinged. Pain shot through her and she gasped, then stumbled and landed on her rear end. She knocked against the feed barrel and it fell over. Straightening slowly, the pain eased and Becca let out a slow breath. "Okay, let's not move that way again."

Jack bounded in beside her, and she scratched his ears while she waited for the spasm to pass.

Nathan appeared in the doorway. "Did you say something?" He frowned. "Are you okay?"

"Yes, I just moved wrong and my back's letting me know it's not happy about it."

He nodded to the mess on the floor. "You knocked over the barrel. Let me get a shovel and I'll help clean it up."

"That's all right. I've got it."

"Won't take but a few minutes."

He disappeared and she sighed. A glint of white in the midst of the feed caught her attention. She brushed the food away and snagged the item. A plastic bag full of white powder? What?

Cold reality hit her.

"What's that?" Nathan asked. He stood in the doorway, holding the shovel.

"I don't know. It was in the feed."

He took it from her. "It's sealed tight. Like it was done in a factory." His gaze slowly lifted to meet hers.

She frowned. "What does that mean? Is it drugs?"

A hard light entered his eyes and his features tightened. "I don't know, Becca. You tell me."

The words slipped out of his mouth before he could recall them. Her flinch indicated they'd hit their mark and remorse filled him. He didn't want to hurt her. He didn't believe her capable of dealing drugs. In spite of the evidence in front of him.

Becca stood slowly, hand pressing against her lower back. "You think I had something to do with that?"

"I don't know." *No!* he wanted to shout, but his ex-fiancée's betrayal came screaming back at him. Visuals of her in the crack house flit through his mind, the paralyzing shock he felt when he'd realized she was a part of the group he was sent to round up and arrest.

He hadn't wanted to believe her capable, either. And yet, she had been. The hurt on Becca's face nearly killed him.

"How can you not know?" Becca asked. "How can you really believe that I would have anything to do with those drugs?"

"I didn't believe my ex-fiancée could have anything to do with them, either."

But there'd been signs.

He was a cop. A *drug* cop.

He told himself he'd been completely blind to what was right before his nose until she'd been arrested, but that wasn't exactly true. There'd been the whispered phone conversations with people she'd claimed were from work, the agitated behavior that she'd brushed off as stress from dealing with clients.

He'd seen it and chosen to ignore it.

He wouldn't do that again.

But with Becca, there'd been no erratic behavior, no weird phone calls, no slipping away to meet people she didn't want him to meet. Instead of turning a blind eye to certain things, was he refusing to see the truth in Becca?

"Get out," she said, her voice low.

"Becca, don't—"

"I don't want you here. I don't know where these came from. I don't know who put them here, but it wasn't me."

"She said that, too."

She shook her head. "You have some serious baggage to overcome when it comes to that woman."

"No, I'm over her."

"Maybe so, but you're not over the hurt she inflicted on you. The inability to see past what happened and realize that not everyone is like her."

Was she right? Nathan's thoughts swirled. This was Becca. She wouldn't do this.

But he'd been wrong before. What if he was wrong this time, too? Could he risk it? Could he *not* risk it?

She pulled her cell phone from her pocket. "Now, I'm going to call Clay and tell him what's going on."

A dull thud against the back of his head sent pain shattering through his skull. Darkness danced in front of him and Nathan's legs gave out. He went to the ground and heard Becca scream his name.

"Nathan!" She watched him fall and hurried to him, her hands automatically ready to examine him.

She dropped to his side and cradled his face.

"Don't worry, I'm calling 911. I have my phone right here."

Blood pooled beneath his head, soaking the dirt floor.

"Drop it."

The voice registered and she jerked her gaze from Nathan's still form to find herself looking at the barrel of a wicked-looking gun.

"Drop the phone and move away from Nathan."

"Zeb? What are you doing? He needs help."

"If I didn't want him to die, I wouldn't have hit him in the head. Now move!"

Shock held her motionless. Then the fury built, like a slow storm.

"It's you," she whispered. Visuals of him in the barn, always around, in the feed room offering to change out her bins for her. The memories clicked and it all became so clear. How had she missed it? Because she'd thought he was hanging around so much due to his feelings for her. Shame at her assumptions filled her. She brushed it off. He'd let her think that on purpose.

"It's me," he said. "Now, where are the other barrels?"

"What other barrels?"

"The other feed barrels! There were two in the back of this bunch!"

Concern for Nathan wanted to push out every other thought, but she had to focus. Zeb had a gun.

"I—I don't have them anymore."

He blanched. "Not the answer I want. Where are they?"

"I gave them away."

"Gave them away!" His screech reverberated. "To who?"

"A friend who needed some feed for her horses until her order came in!" Becca couldn't help the wobble in her voice. This was Zeb. *How* had she not seen it?

He tossed a backpack at her feet. "Put the drugs in there and let's go."

"What? No! I have to take care of Nathan."

Zeb swung the weapon and aimed it at Nathan. "Do it, or I'll put a bullet in his head. I didn't shoot him when I could have. He has a chance to live if you do exactly what I say."

He was serious. Completely, deadly serious. With a lingering look at Nathan's colorless face, Becca knew the only way she was going to have a chance to help him was to do what Zeb ordered. Zeb hadn't shot Nathan when he could have. Why? He didn't care if he lived or died. It was because he needed her cooperation. As long as there was a chance to help Nathan, she would do whatever Zeb wanted her to do. He'd use that to his advantage.

She grabbed the backpack and scrambled through the spilled feed to find the bags of drugs.

"Make sure you get them all."

"How many are there?"

"Fifty."

"Fifty bags of what? Cocaine? Heroin?"

"Doesn't matter. Just get busy."

"What was your purpose in everything? Why did you try to kill me?"

"Why couldn't you have just died the day you fell off Pete?" he muttered.

She paused and glanced at Nathan. His eyes were still closed, but his chest rose and fell in a steady rhythm. "What did you do to Pete?"

"Laced his water with a bit of cocaine."

Fury gathered beneath the fear. "What about Pete's abscess? I saw that with my own eyes."

"I knew you'd go looking into why Pete was acting so crazy. I gave him that wound and called it an abscess." He shook his head. "You didn't even question it."

No, she hadn't. She'd been so consumed with her own healing, she hadn't been as focused as she should have been. And she'd trusted Zeb. "You're a good vet. Animals love you." She shot him a withering glance. "What a waste."

Her look didn't faze him. "Nope, a good cover."

She continued to load the backpack, not sure whether to pray that Nathan would wake up or stay out. She was afraid if he woke, Zeb would hurt him again. Or worse.

Finally, Becca counted the last packet and shoved the bag at Zeb. He took it and slung it over his shoulder.

A memory flashed in her mind. "You were here. In the barn."

"What?"

"The day of my accident." Or murder attempt. She bit her tongue on the words. No sense in provoking him. "You were here in the barn."

"Yes. You weren't supposed to be here, remember?"

The memory returned full force and she gasped. "I do remember now." She'd had an appointment with the banker and she'd changed it so she could do the lesson with Christina. She simply hadn't been up to facing what she knew he was going to tell her. She knew her financial status and didn't need it hammered home that she was skating on thin ice. "I asked you what you were doing, and you said you'd left some piece of equipment and had come back to get it."

"Right. But I couldn't tell if you believed me or not."

She blinked. "Why wouldn't I believe you?"

Zeb didn't speak.

"Must have been your guilty conscience."

"I don't have a conscience anymore." He motioned to the door with the weapon. "Let's go."

"Where?"

"To make my promised delivery. If you had just been ten minutes later getting here, I would have had this all taken care of and you wouldn't be in this situation. But no," he muttered. "You had to drive up just as I was getting ready to transfer the drugs."

"Did you kill Larry? The one who was shot sitting in the back of Clay's cruiser?"

He scowled. "It doesn't matter."

"Of course it matters! He was a person."

"A person who got caught and could take us all down."

"Who else, Zeb?"

"I've said too much. Now let's go."

"What does it matter how much you say? You're not going to let me live anyway."

Her soft words seemed to reach some forgotten part of him and he flinched. Then his features hardened and he grabbed her arm to shove her toward the barn exit. "Now."

Nathan still lay quiet on the hay, blood congealing beneath his head. How her fingers itched to examine the wound, clean it, bandage it…kiss it. Nathan!

Her heart pounded against her ribs and she scrambled

for an escape idea. With her back, she couldn't attack him and have a hope of overpowering him. She'd simply wind up more hurt than she already was. Possibly to the point that she wouldn't be able to move. No, she had to be smart. To think.

Zeb stuck a hand in his pocket and withdrew a lighter.

Becca sucked in a terrified breath. "Zeb. Don't. Please don't burn it down."

"Sorry, Becca. I have to destroy any evidence that I might have left here."

He wasn't sorry.

"Then at least help me get Nathan out."

He gave a harsh laugh. "I don't think so."

Her terror intensified. "I'm not leaving him."

"Yes, you are. I might need a hostage and you're the best option I've got right now."

"Everyone knows you're here frequently. Even if you have left something behind no one would think anything about it. You don't have to burn it down."

He flicked the lighter and held it against the hay bale. Grief and fury flared inside her. But she didn't move, just watched the flame.

"I'm not going with you."

Zeb turned the gun on Nathan. "If you don't come peacefully, I'll put a bullet in his head." He shrugged. "If you come nicely, you never know. He might wake up and get out."

If he really thought there was a chance Nathan was going to escape, he'd never just walk away. But his words held truth in one sense. Nathan wouldn't get up with a bullet in his head.

She knelt beside him while smoke filled the air

around her. "Nathan! Wake up!" Zeb grabbed her upper arm and dragged her toward the exit.

"The horses!"

"Collateral damage! Gotta look like an accident."

An accident. And then they'd find her body somewhere in a ditch.

"Nathan!"

The horses whinnied and started to panic. She heard their frantic hooves beating against their stalls and her heart cried while her feet moved. Zeb held her bicep in a vice grip, and there was no pulling away from him. And she couldn't take a chance on severely incapacitating herself by fighting him. Right now her back hurt, but it wouldn't keep her from running if she had the opportunity.

"Nathan!"

Flames licked at her heels as the two of them burst from the building.

FIFTEEN

Nathan lay on the dirt floor of the barn until he knew Zeb and Becca were gone. He'd never fully lost consciousness, but he lay still long enough for the ringing in his ears and the throbbing in his head to subside a bit.

And as long as Zeb thought he was dead—or dying in the fire—Nathan might live. And he had to live in order to make sure Becca survived.

At least she was now out of the barn even though her cries still echoed in his ears. The head wound wasn't lethal, just painful. A possible concussion, but at least he could move. He thought.

Once they were out of sight, Nathan rolled carefully onto his right side and then to his stomach. The smoke grew thicker and the flames roared stronger, licking up everything in their path.

Horses cried out, their hooves slashing against their stalls that had now become their death traps.

Nathan army-crawled to the nearest stall, ignoring the renewed pounding in his head that the movement triggered. At least his vision wasn't blurry even though he had to squint to see through the haze of smoke.

Pulling himself up, staying out of the way of the exit, he released the latch on the first stall. Pete raced out.

The temperature in the barn climbed. Sweat dripped into his eyes and down his forehead, and he swiped it away with his wrist.

His lungs strained and his eyes burned.

He made his way down the line of stalls, one by one, releasing the animals, hurrying, desperate to stay ahead of the flames.

Smoke clogged his lungs and Nathan coughed into his elbow. Finally, strength ebbing, at the last stall, he took a breath near the floor then stood. He released the latch and caught the horse by the mane as it came out. With a low grunt and a last-ditch, life-saving, effort, he swung himself onto the animal's back.

The fire continued to burn along the opposite wall, but thankfully, the path out of the barn remained flame free.

Nathan ducked his head and let the horse find his way out.

Once out in the open and away from the burning barn, Nathan pulled the horse to a reluctant stop and slid from the animal's back, dragging in deep gulps of fresh air.

His legs buckled and nausea churned. Coughing, he reached for his phone and slapped an empty pocket. With a groan, he rolled to his knees. *Becca…*

"Nathan!" Becca tried to run back toward the barn, but Zeb kept a firm grip on her upper arm. She jerked against his hold, turning to fight him, and he gave her a hard shake. Hard enough to send warning spasms up her spine.

"He's dead by now! Keep walking! Get in the truck! You're going to take me to those barrels."

Becca stumbled and went to her knees, grief stabbing her. "Nathan!"

He yanked her to her feet. "Go!"

Horses thundered past and her heart leapt. Was it possible Nathan had managed to let them out? Or had they broken down the stalls in their fear and desperation to escape?

Please let it be Nathan, God. With hope partially renewed, she walked on shaky legs, staying just ahead of Zeb and the gun he jabbed into the small of her back.

"Where are the barrels?"

"I told you. I gave them away." But Jean hadn't called to let her know that she'd found anything unusual in them. Like bags of drugs. So maybe she hadn't gotten that far down into the barrel of feed yet?

Becca turned back toward the burning barn and horror filled her anew. There was no way Nathan had survived. Even if he'd managed to let the horses out, he couldn't have gotten himself out, could he?

"You killed him," she whispered.

"Hopefully. Now, the barrels! I want to know where they are. If I don't get those drugs back, I'm a dead man, understand?"

"I understand, but I'm not siccing you on one of my friends." She shrugged, tears dripping off her chin. "I simply won't do it."

"Then you're dead. I can find out who it was by simple process of elimination. I walk up to the door and say, 'Hi, Becca wanted to know when you'd be returning her barrels. Oh, I'm sorry, wrong neighbor.' And then move on to the next. So you can make this easier and live a little longer if you help me get them back. And maybe I won't kill the person who has them. Got it?"

Becca got it. It wouldn't take him an hour to figure

it out. Which meant he didn't need her. But he seemed to be in a hurry.

She trembled, tried to think. She had to get back to the barn to get Nathan. No, Nathan was dead. Sobs crowded her throat and she choked them back. She swiped the tears that had escaped and sucked in a breath. Crying wasn't an option.

Maybe Nathan had gotten out. *Please, God, let him have gotten out.*

"The Staffords."

She stiffened. "What?"

"That's who you gave the feed to, isn't it?"

"Why do you think it's them?" Fear clutched her gut. No, she couldn't put Jean and Hank in danger. "Why them? I have quite a few neighbors and friends around here."

"Because I think I remember overhearing her on the phone ordering feed because she was almost out."

He was going to go to Jean's first. "Yes, you're right. It's her. But keep in mind, she hasn't called or said anything about finding drugs in the barrels. She probably hasn't used enough feed yet to find them. You don't have to hurt her."

"I'll play that one by ear. I don't want to hurt her if I don't have to. And as long as you cooperate, I won't have to."

Zeb continued to steer her toward the truck, and she stumbled and let herself fall to the ground, at the same time trying not to injure her back again.

Her move took him by surprise and his hand fell away from her arm. She wrapped her fingers around the large rock and waited for him to bend over to grab her.

As she predicted, his fingers clamped on to her left

arm. She let him pull, got her feet under her, and swung with her right arm as hard as she could.

The rock smashed into the right side of his head. He cried out, the gun tumbling from his fingers. Then his eyes closed and he collapsed on top of the weapon. She wanted to get the gun, but while he might be unconscious, he could be faking it, too.

Becca wasn't finding out. Heart thudding, fear sending tremors through her, she raced back toward the burning barn. "Nathan!"

Nathan scrambled to get his feet under him. The dizziness had eased, but his fear for Becca hadn't. He pushed himself around to the side of the burning barn and saw Becca running toward him. Behind her lay a body on the ground. Zeb.

"Becca!"

"Nathan!"

Zeb stirred, shook his head and looked up to meet Nathan's gaze. The pure fury there chilled him. Nathan had no phone, no weapon and—it was starting to snow. "Come on, Becca. Hurry!"

"What?" She looked back over her shoulder. Nathan saw Zeb pull something from underneath him and realized it was a gun. Ignoring his own throbbing head and queasy stomach, he stumbled toward her and grabbed her hand. A gunshot sounded, but it was a wide miss.

Still, they needed to get to cover. "Into the woods, Becca."

"No. The house. I have the rifle."

"And it's a wide-open path," he said as he pulled her with him. "We'd be sitting ducks."

"But we need help and Zeb made me toss my phone."

Nathan continued to lead her back around the barn.

He felt sure Zeb was following. "We're going to have to make a run for it."

She nodded and hand in hand, they took off for the woods. The crack of the pistol sounded again and this time the bullet only missed him by inches. Nathan swerved and Becca stayed with him. "Zigzag!"

She understood and copied his movements, running in an erratic pattern. Two more bullets whizzed by but missed, and then they were in the protective cover of the trees. Nathan's head throbbed with an intensity that nearly blinded him, but there was nothing to be done except to ignore it. He pressed a hand to the wound and felt the dried blood covering the area. He winced at his touch but figured it could be worse.

"You're hurt," Becca said.

"Yes, but I'll live. As long as we can stay out of the path of Zeb's bullets, we both will."

"We need to get help. Find a phone or something." She stayed with him. "Jean's," she said. "We need to head to Jean's. Zeb will go there. It's only about a mile north of here."

"How do you know he'll go there?" His long legs ate up the distance, but she kept pace with him pretty well.

"Because he guessed that they were the neighbors I gave the feed to."

"Let me guess. Those barrels had drugs in them, too."

"Yes."

"It's all coming together now."

"For me, too."

He squeezed her hand. "I'm sorry I doubted you back there."

"I'm sorry, too. That hurt."

"Yeah. I know."

"But I'll probably forgive you."

"Thanks."

They fell silent and hurried as best they could through the undergrowth, staying just on the border of the tree line but far enough back so no one would be able to see them moving.

Finally, Becca grabbed his hand and pulled him to a stop. "There."

"Where?"

"Through the trees and up the hill and we'll be at Jean's pasture. She has a phone in her barn, but that's probably the first place Zeb will look for the barrels."

"Then we need to see if we can beat him there."

SIXTEEN

Becca raced with Nathan toward Jean's barn. "We've got to warn her." Fear for her friend had a tight grip on her heart, and she just couldn't seem to go fast enough. "We have to get there." She stumbled and only his lightning-fast action kept her from going down.

He helped her get her balance. "Take it easy. Be careful."

"Right."

The field was rocky and uneven. It would be easy to fall. She slowed her pace even though her heart pounded in her ears and fear urged her on.

They crossed the property and had just reached the edge of the Stafford's barn when the sound of an engine caught her ears. Nathan pulled her to a stop. "Do you hear that?"

"Yes. Look." Zeb's truck had just turned into the driveway. Jean opened the door and stepped out onto the porch. From her vantage point, Becca could see the front door, but unless Jean was looking for her, she probably wouldn't notice her by the barn.

"Stay back," Nathan said. "Don't let Zeb know we're here."

"He's going to hurt her."

"Not if he can help it. Can you slip into the barn and call for help while I watch him?"

"I'll try. Make sure he doesn't hurt Jean, please."

"They're just talking right now. I think if he can get what he needs without alerting her, he won't do anything to hurt her. But if he knows we're here…"

"Right."

"Go. Hurry."

Becca slipped into the open door of the barn and went straight to the office. She'd been in the barn several times and was familiar with the layout.

Only Jean had locked the office door. "Oh Jean, help me out here," she whispered. "I know you have a key somewhere."

Becca ran her fingers along the trim above the door and breathed a sigh of relief when she knocked the small silver key from its hiding place.

She heard a yell from outside the barn and froze for a second before adrenaline and fear shot her into action.

With shaking hands, she grabbed the key from the dirt floor and opened the office door. Snagging the cordless phone from the base, she dialed 911. Only to hold it to her ear and realize she had no dial tone. What? Zeb hadn't gotten here in time to cut the line, so…

Becca stilled and closed her eyes, trying to think. Well, there was nothing else she could do except try to sneak into the house and use the phone in the kitchen.

Footsteps fell outside the office and she froze for a split second.

"I figured you'd head here first," Zeb said from behind her.

Becca spun to find Zeb holding a terrified Jean, his arm wrapped around the base of her throat, gun pressed to her temple. Nathan stood slightly in front of both of them, his jaw tight, nostrils flaring. He held his hands in a surrender position, and Becca knew it had to be because Zeb had threatened Jean. But why had Nathan revealed himself?

Zeb motioned with his head and said to Nathan, "Get over there with her."

Nathan moved without protest to stand in front of Becca. While she appreciated his desire to protect her, there was still Jean. "Let her go, Zeb. She has a sick husband to take care of."

He shoved the woman away from him and she stumbled against Nathan. Nathan steadied her and stepped toward Zeb.

"Anyone that comes out of this office gets a bullet."

Why not just shoot them now? she wondered.

Because he might need a hostage if he didn't find what he was looking for.

Zeb shut the door.

Nathan turned to her and Jean. "Are you two okay?"

Jean nodded. "Scared to death, but not physically hurt."

"Same here," Becca said. "How's your head?"

"Throbbing."

"I called the police," Jean said. "I heard the gunshots and because of all the trouble over at your place, I figured you might need some help."

"Oh, bless you," Becca said. "I couldn't get a dial tone on your cordless."

Jean grimaced. "I disconnected the landline last month. We just didn't use it that much and I decided to save money on it. Sorry about that."

"It's okay. Are they sending someone?"

"The dispatcher took the message, but I don't know how serious she thought the situation was."

"Once Clay hears, he'll take it seriously," Becca said.

"In the meantime, I've got to get out of here and stop Zeb," Nathan murmured. He looked around. "No windows." He tried the door and while it opened slightly, it refused to go any farther. "He's got the door jammed."

Becca grabbed the shovel from the nail on the wall. "Can you use this?"

"I can try."

Nathan slid the end into the small crack and used the handle as a lever. The door popped open.

And a bullet pinged off the molding.

Nathan ducked and pulled back inside the small room. "Well, no one's going out that way. The feed room is just diagonal to this one, so he can see the door while he works on the barrels." He turned and ran his fingers along the wall. "This leads outside, doesn't it? It's the outside wall."

Jean nodded, her pale face stark against her black T-shirt. "And to think I chose this room because it didn't have windows. I was afraid someone might want to break inside if they saw my desk and laptop."

"Is it okay if I try to kick a hole in the wall?" Nathan asked.

"Please," Jean said. "Anything to get out of this."

It was wood, but the question was, how heavy was it?

Nathan leaned on the board. "Plywood," he said. "Nailed between two-by-fours. I may not have to kick it, just push it hard enough to loosen it from the nails."

"Yes. Hank was going to finish this room and put insulation in but hasn't felt up to doing it yet."

"Okay, stand back." Nathan pressed both palms against the plywood and gave it a hard push. It shivered but didn't release. He leaned harder and felt the nails start to give. With steady pressure, he continued to separate the plywood from the two-by-fours. Slowly, inch by squeaky inch, the board gave way. Nathan finally gave it one last shove and the piece fell to the ground. "Run up to the house and call Clay, Becca. Be quiet and quick. I'm going to keep an eye on Zeb and see what's what."

Nathan didn't wait for her agreement or argument, he simply slipped out of the hole in the wall, staying close to the building. He figured Zeb was in the stall where the feed barrels were, gathering his stash. For a moment, Nathan took inventory of his wounds and decided he could take the man down in spite of the headache still pounding at the back of his skull.

He edged around the side of the barn and trotted up to the open door. How he wished he had his weapon. Moving quickly, but silently, he stepped inside the barn and grabbed a feed bucket from the wall. Not the best weapon, but it would have to do. All of Jean's tools, rakes, shovels and other barn equipment were locked up.

Nathan stood and listened. Every few seconds, he'd hear a quiet thump. Zeb making sure he got every last bag. Nathan started to enter the room when another voice brought him up short. "I can't believe you were so stupid. You got it all?"

"It's not my fault," Zeb protested. "I didn't give the barrels away."

"Whatever. Let's get this stuff and get out of here."

"What about the three locked in the office?"

"Shoot them or burn the place down, Just get rid of them."

Nathan pulled back. There was no way he could take on two men. Not in his weakened condition.

A sound behind him jerked his attention around.

Clay stepped inside, his finger lifted to his lips. Nathan had never been so glad to see someone in his life. He nodded and moved back.

"Got it," the other man said. "Let's get out of here. You got a lighter?"

"Yeah."

"Take care of it and meet me in the truck."

The man with the voice Nathan didn't recognize stepped out of the feed area. When he saw them, he pulled up short and raised his weapon.

Clay's gun cracked and the man fell.

Zeb bolted from the room and took off for the back door of the barn. Nathan went after him, dove and clipped him around the knees. They both went down.

Zeb rolled and came up swinging.

Nathan ducked and threw a punch that held every ounce of anger and pain that boiled inside of him.

Satisfaction swept over him when Zeb's eyes rolled back in his head and the man went limp.

Becca lowered the pitchfork and leaned against the wall. She and Jean had crawled through the hole in the wall after Nathan. Jean had headed for the house and the phone, but there was no way Becca was going to let him face Zeb on his own.

And when Zeb had burst from the feed room and headed her way, she'd been determined to stop him no matter what it took. Fortunately, Nathan had managed to tackle him. And knock him out.

"That was quite a punch," she said.

Nathan shook out his fist and winced. "I think I might have cracked a knuckle or two." He glanced at the unconscious man. "But it was worth it. Are you two okay?"

"We're fine."

It hit her.

It was over.

Her breath whooshed out of her lungs and her knees went weak. Nathan hurried over and caught her before she hit the ground. "Sit."

"Yes, I think that might be a good idea."

He lowered her to the floor while Clay pulled a zip tie around Zeb's wrists. The other man lay moaning behind him, but he had cuffs on so Becca wasn't worried about him doing any more damage. "Who is he?" Clay asked. "I don't recognize him."

"I do," Becca said. "His name is Ray Foster. He recently started boarding his horse with me. Although, I'm sure that was just a way to gain easy access to my property."

"Yeah." Clay had called for backup. Lance and Parker Little arrived within seconds of each other. Zeb was starting to stir. "I look forward to getting a search warrant for this guy's place and seeing what turns up."

"I'm ready for him to be off my property," Jean said.

Clay nodded to Lance to grab under one arm while he got the other. Together they hefted him out to the cruiser and Parker helped Foster to his feet. He led the grumbling man out. "I'm going to need statements from you three."

"We'll come down tomorrow and do it," Nathan said.

Jean raked a hand through her hair and blinked as though coming out of a daze.

Becca pulled herself together enough to walk over and hug her friend. "I'm so sorry about all this."

"Oh, honey, it's not your fault. I'm just glad it all ended well with no one seriously hurt."

"Yes, me, too."

"I'm going to check on Hank." Jean gave her one last squeeze then headed for her house. Her husband was coming down the steps, dressed in pajamas and holding a rifle. "Everything all right out here? I heard a gunshot." He frowned at the sight before him. "What's going on?"

"Just a little bit of craziness, but everything's fine now," she said, steering him back inside. "Come on and I'll fill you in."

Nathan slid an arm around her shoulders and pulled her to him. "I'm sorry for everything."

"Like what?"

"Like coming here under false pretenses. Sort of. I really did want to help you."

"Clay asked you to investigate me, didn't he?"

"Yeah."

She sighed. "That's what you were doing in my office, too, huh?"

"Yep."

"I should be mad at you."

"Furious, really."

She gave a half laugh, half sob. "But I think I'm just going to be grateful to be alive and be done with it."

"I'm totally on board with that plan."

Becca leaned into him and kissed him. "I think I'm falling in love with you, Nathan Williams."

His eyes went wide, and he blinked a few times before his lips split in a wide grin. "Really?"

"Yes, really."

"If my head didn't hurt so bad, I'd grab you up and spin you in a circle."

"And if my back didn't hurt so bad, I'd let you."

He laughed. "We're a pair, aren't we?"

She sobered. "We could be."

This time he kissed her soundly. A long, tender kiss that spoke of deep feelings on both sides. Neither wanted it to end, but he finally lifted his head and sighed. "I'm glad you think you're falling in love with me, Becca. Because I think the feeling is mutual."

"You think?"

He smiled. "I loved you in high school with a teenage boy crush. What I feel for you now is similar, but different. Much stronger and longer lasting. But could we go out on a few dates and get to know each other more without having to worry about someone shooting at us?"

Another laugh escaped her. "I'm okay with doing that."

"You want to go see Brody Mac and make sure he's okay?"

"Absolutely."

Nathan didn't particularly care for hospitals, and this one housed a man who'd hurt Becca deeply. After they'd been able to leave the scene of Jean's barn, he'd taken Becca home to wash her face and clean up a little. She'd also cleaned his head wound and given him three stitches. "Do you always have medical supplies lying around?"

She'd laughed. "Always. Occupational hazard."

While she'd gotten ready to go see Brody Mac, Nathan had the wild idea that he could do one more good deed for the day. He hoped his last-minute phone call would bear fruit, but there was no way to know for sure. All he could do was wait and see. They walked through the entrance and got Brody Mac's room number.

Together they rode the elevator and stepped off on the fourth floor. "This way," Nathan said, taking her hand.

He liked that holding hands with her was as natural as breathing.

It didn't take long to find Brody Mac's room.

Becca pulled up short when she saw Mr. MacDougal standing outside. He looked at her and scowled, but stepped aside. "He's been asking for you."

Nathan placed a hand at the small of her back and they took that as permission to enter. They slipped around the still-frowning man and into the room.

Mrs. MacDougal sat at her son's side, holding his hand. When Brody Mac saw them, his eyes lit up in spite of his pale face that said he wasn't feeling well at all. "Becca, you came to see me."

Becca crossed the room and took his other hand. "Of course I did. I couldn't let my best worker be in the hospital without a visit, now could I?"

"No, you really couldn't."

Becca grinned and looked at Mrs. MacDougal. "Hi."

The woman offered a wan smile. "Hi."

She was younger than Nathan expected. Maybe early forties.

"How're you doing, Brody Mac?" she asked.

"My head hurts, but they have medicine to make it feel better. It hurts like yours, Becca. You know, the hurt that makes you want to puke?"

She squeezed his hand. "I know it well. You have my sympathies and prayers, then."

"Thanks, I need them."

"He was unconscious when they brought him," Mrs. MacDougal said, "but he woke up fairly quickly and that pleased the doctors."

Brody Mac frowned. "I went looking for you, Becca, but Dr. Zeb was in the barn doing something in the feed room. I asked him what he was doing and he yelled at me." His lower lip trembled. "He acted like my daddy and it scared me so I ran."

"I'm sorry, Brody Mac. I'm sure that was super scary."

"But the other man told me to come back."

He had to be referring to Ray Foster.

"Did you go back?"

"No way. I was getting out of there. I got the moped and zoomed off, but one of them started chasing me on Pete! And then I heard a loud pop and my head exploded." He touched it and grimaced. "Well, not really, but it sure felt like it."

Nathan curled his fingers into a fist and wished he could smash Zeb's face one more time.

"It's okay now," Becca told him. "You're safe and are going to heal right up. Soon you'll be back with the horses."

"Are they okay?"

"They're just fine and waiting for you to get back to them."

He smiled, not his usual buoyant grin, but he would have to heal some before that returned.

His mother turned the television to a sitcom and handed Brody the remote. To Nathan and Becca, she said, "Can we talk over there in the corner?"

"Of course."

Nathan met Becca's gaze and she shrugged. They moved into the short hallway that led to the door. Mrs. MacDougal spoke low. "Did they catch who did this?"

"Yes, ma'am. They did."

"So it was the vet? Zeb?"

"Yes," Becca said. "I'm so sorry I didn't try to keep Brody Mac away from the ranch. I knew it could be dangerous, but I was afraid if I told him to stay away, he'd sneak back on anyway."

"He would have," the woman said. "This isn't your fault. I'm just grateful he's okay and the man who did it was caught."

Becca hugged her. "Let me know if there's anything I can do to help."

"I will. Thank you for everything."

"And Mr. MacDougal? Is he…" She trailed off and Nathan figured she wasn't quite sure how to phrase her question.

Brody Mac's mother smiled. A small, weary tug of her lips. Then she shrugged. "He seemed pretty shaken up with the whole thing. Will it make a difference in how he treats Brody Mac? I don't know. I have hope, I guess."

"Well, he didn't yell at me when he saw me, so that's progress," Becca said.

They all three laughed, and Nathan and Becca said their goodbyes. Outside in the hallway, Nathan didn't see Mr. MacDougal, but he did see another man he'd been hoping would show up.

Becca spotted her father as she stepped out of the room. She jerked to a halt and swallowed against the sudden surge of nervousness. "Dad?"

"I heard you were going to be here."

"Yes. Just visiting a friend."

He nodded. "I…ah…could we go to my office and talk for a few minutes?"

She hesitated only a second, then shrugged. "Sure."

With a short nod, her father turned on his heel and led the way down the hall. Nathan took her hand and she latched on, needing his strength.

Once inside his office, he shut the door and motioned for them to take a seat. Becca took one seat and Nathan the other while her father rounded the desk to lower himself into his plush leather chair. "Ah...thank you. For agreeing to talk to me."

"What is it, Dad?" He was acting incredibly weird.

"I called Clay Starke and talked to him after your mother raked me over the coals and told me I was being ridiculous in this endeavor to get you to come back to medicine."

She blinked. "Oh. Okay."

"Clay told me you had a couple of near misses, that someone was trying to kill you."

"I believe I told you that."

"Actually, you told me you thought it might be me."

"Well, yes. I did. Tell you that, I mean. I never really fully believed it, but..."

He nodded. "But you believed it enough that you felt like you had to ask me about it. The knowledge that you could believe something like that...hurt and—"

He was hurt?

Anger rose hot and swift. "Really? I hurt *you*? You have the nerve to sit there and tell me that—" She broke off for a nanosecond before jabbing a finger at him. "Try being your daughter and believing you would do something like that. Try being kicked out of the family and separated from your parents for an entire year. Try falling off a horse and being seriously hurt and your parents don't even care enough—" She would *not* cry. Fury boiled and she stood to plant both hands on his desk while she leaned toward him. Complete shock held him still. And no wonder. She'd never spoken to him this way, but she could no more keep the words from tumbling from her lips than she could stop the earth's rotation. "Try working your tail off night and day, trying to make a dream come true—a dream that you would love to share with your parents but can't because they're too wrapped up in their own selfishness to—"

Nathan's hand on her arm brought her words to an abrupt halt. She turned to face him and thought she saw a bit of pride in his eyes. "Ah, Becca, why don't you just listen to what he has to say?"

"Why should I?"

"Because you need to."

Becca turned to look at her father and this time saw past the red in her vision. He almost looked…proud. Maybe even a tad amused. She stamped a foot. "What's so funny?"

"You look just like your mother when she's ready to hang someone high and dry in the courtroom."

Becca lifted her chin. "I think I like that comparison." She lowered herself back into the chair while she drew in a steadying breath. She'd really gone off on him and shame started to creep in. He was her father, after all. She cleared her throat. "Sorry, I've had a lot of emotions over the last year when it comes to you and Mom, and I guess I…ah…well, go ahead. Say what you need to say."

"Like I was saying, I talked to Clay." His expression sobered. "Clay made it plain that you could have died several times. I have to say, I can hardly wrap my mind around it."

"Try being the target," she muttered.

His gaze met hers. "I'm not a man who is easy to get along with, Rebecca. I know that. You know that." He waved a hand. "Everyone who knows me knows that. But," he leaned forward, "and I'm going to say this in front of your young man here. I love you and I don't want to lose you." His voice dropped on that last word and Becca sat still, stunned, still hearing those three words she'd longed to hear from him all her life echoing in her mind. *I love you.*

Did he really?

As though he could read her thoughts, he drew in a shaky breath. "I really do, Becca. I've behaved… shamefully. There's no excuse for it other than…pride. I hope we can start over as I can't go on with things the way they are between us. And frankly, neither can your mother. I've been too hardheaded and proud, and I'm working on trying to be less of both."

The anger left in an instant. Love for the man rushed in. Becca rose and walked around to stand in front of her father. He stood and she slipped her arms around his waist. "I love you, too, Dad."

He hugged her. An awkward hug with a clumsy pat on her shoulder, but it was a start.

She released him and stepped back. "Thank you."

He cleared his throat. "So, will we see you at Julianna and Ross's for Christmas?"

"Yes," she said as she tried to control her ragged emotions. "Yes, you will."

He looked at Nathan. "And you?"

"I wouldn't miss it."

SEVENTEEN

Christmas Day

"Are you ready?" Nathan called from the front door.

"I'm coming!" Becca grabbed a pie from the kitchen counter and hurried into the foyer. She placed the dessert onto the small side table and grabbed Nathan's outstretched hand. He thought she'd been about to hand him the dessert, but she had something else in mind. "Come here for a second."

Curiosity lighting his eyes, he clasped her fingers and let her lead him into the den. His gaze immediately landed on the fireplace—and the decoration that finished out the mantel.

His stocking on the end next to hers.

"What do you think?"

He turned to her and lifted her chin. The emotion in his eyes caused her throat to tighten with her own feelings. "I think it's just perfect. Thanks, Becca." He spied the empty paper bag she'd tossed to the side. "Wait a minute. Is that what you had to stop and get at the gift shop in the hospital?"

"Yep. I saw it in the window and knew it was the one."

"I think you're the one."

Her heart warmed at his husky words and she stepped forward to wrap her arms around his neck. His hands settled on her waist and he leaned over to kiss her. Sweetly, gently, with a restraint that touched her. He stepped back and cleared his throat. "So, ah, I know we've only been on a few dates since that afternoon in Jean's barn where you decided not to be mad at me and we both were thinking along the same lines."

"Thinking what?"

He tickled a rib and she squealed. "Don't do that."

"I told you I was thinking I was falling in love with you, and you said you were thinking the same thing."

"Oh. That thinking. I think I said it first, though."

"Yes. Well, whatever. We were both thinking it and that's all that matters. What I'm trying to say is that I'd still like to go on a few more dates with you."

She offered him a confused frown. Where was he going with this? He knew she'd go on however many dates he wanted to go on. "Okay. I'd like that, too."

Then he reached into the front pocket of his jeans and pulled out a small box. Becca gasped as her heart dropped into her stomach. He lowered himself to one knee and the butterflies broke out in full force. She pressed a hand to her middle as though that would help. "Nathan?"

"Like I said, I'd like to go on a few more dates, but I'd like to go on them with my ring on your finger. If you could possibly want that, too. I know it's a bit quick, but I love you, Becca. You're one of the most intriguing, inspiring, amazing people I've ever known. And I'd be honored if you'd marry me."

She couldn't hold back the tears anymore, and she couldn't seem to speak. So she simply nodded and sniffed. Then laughed. He held the ring so she could see it. "It's beautiful."

"I sort of snooped in your jewelry box the other day and found one of your rings. I measured it so I'd know your size so I hope it fits." He removed the teardrop diamond from the box and took her hand in his. A fine tremor ran through her fingers, but his touch warmed her. He slid the ring on her finger and then brought it to his lips to place a kiss on it. "'Til death do us part?"

She found her voice. "I thought death might come before the marriage part, to be honest, but yes, 'til death do us part." She once again threw herself into his arms and he lifted her gently off her feet to kiss her. When he placed her back on the floor, she cupped his chin. "I'll never get tired of that."

"Ditto."

She stilled. "But what about your job in Nashville."

"Yeah. About that." He scratched his chin. "Well, it seems like Wrangler's Corner is growing by leaps and bounds. You've seen the construction for the new grocery store that just started, not to mention the new gas station that's going in on the corner of Main and South, and then there's the huge subdivision that's just been approved." He shrugged. "Clay said he has two deputy positions that have just opened up with funding and everything. He asked if I was interested."

"And are you?"

"I am. If you are, that is. Interested in me staying in Wrangler's Corner."

"Oh, I'm interested."

"It won't be as much money as I was making in Nashville, but it won't be as much stress, either. And I'm ready for a new place to make new memories."

Tears welled and one slid down her cheek. He swiped

it away for her then kissed her again. "Why don't we just hang out here today?" she asked. "We can build a fire and eat pie for lunch."

Nathan laughed. "No way. I don't want to make your family mad at me before we're even married. We're going to the Starkes' for at least a little while." He sniffed. "But that pie does smell amazing. Let's get to Aunt Julianna and Uncle Ross's so I can eat it. Do you think they'll hate me forever if I refuse to share?"

She laughed. "Yes, probably. They love my pies."

"Okay, then after it's all over, we can come back here, build a fire, and eat pie for dinner."

"I love that plan."

"And I love you."

After another sweet kiss, they walked out the door, Jack at their heels, and climbed into Nathan's truck. He reached over with his right hand and snagged her fingers. "My parents are going to be passing back through Wrangler's Corner around New Year's, and I asked them to make sure they stay a couple of days. They agreed. I was hoping we could all spend some time together while they're here."

She grinned. "That would be lovely. It'll be nice to see them again."

When they arrived to her aunt and uncle's house, it was already a magnificent madhouse with children running in and out of the house, laughing and yelling at top volume. With the weather in the midsixties and sunny, everyone else was taking advantage of it and hanging around outside, either on the porch or in the big yard.

Love for her crazy, wonderful family filled her. She and Nathan climbed from the truck and Nathan grabbed the pie.

Her father left the porch swing and was the first

one to greet her with a hug while her mother looked on with a teary smile. "You're getting better at that," Becca whispered.

He laughed and flushed, his eyes sparkling in a way she'd never seen before. She knew he would never leave his precious work for long, but Becca could tell he was learning to appreciate what was important in life. "I've…ah…contracted someone to rebuild your barn. And I'm paying for it."

Becca froze, her heart thudding into the bottom of her shoes. "Dad—"

He held up a hand. "Let me rephrase." He placed a hand over his heart and cleared his throat. "Becca, I'd like to rebuild your barn for you, and I'd like to do it with no strings attached. I promise. I simply want to help."

"Even if it means I may never return to medicine?"

He winced. She knew he couldn't help it. Then he cleared his throat. "Yes. Even if you never come back to medicine. And you can design the whole thing. Cost isn't a factor so keep that in mind when you're working on it."

For a moment, she searched his eyes, then met Nathan's. He gave her a slight nod. She returned the nod as joy broke free within her. "Okay, Dad. Insurance will only take care of so much, and there are some improvements I'd like to make, so thank you. That would be amazing. Beyond amazing. It would be an answer to my prayers."

He grinned. "Great! This will be a new beginning for us, okay?"

She nodded and bit her lip against the tears that wanted to come. Happy tears, but she didn't want to ruin her makeup.

Her father turned to Nathan. "Now, son, if you want to hand me that pie, I'll take it inside for you."

Handing it over, Nathan laughed. "Right. Try not to eat it before you reach the front door."

With a wink, he took off.

"Becca! You're here!" Sabrina gathered her in a hug along with her crew of children. Little Hannah wasn't so little anymore.

"She's grown a foot since I last saw her!" Becca said, and leaned over to plop a kiss on the child's head before she darted for the door after her older siblings.

With a grin, Sabrina nodded. "She's going to be tall like her daddy."

Seth and Tonya, who looked ready to pop at any moment, walked toward them. Sabrina laughed and patted her sister-in-law's belly. "You think you'll make it through lunch?"

Tonya rolled her eyes. "It wouldn't bother me in the least not to, but I still have three weeks to go. And I'm supposed to be on bed rest, so on that note, I'm going to find a seat and put my feet up." She looked at Seth. "Feel free to bring me a plate wherever I might land because once I'm down, I don't plan on getting up for a while. At least not without a crane."

"Yes, ma'am. My pleasure."

Tonya waddled toward the door and Seth shook his head. He hugged Becca then looked at Nathan with one of those looks that only guys understood. Nathan grinned. "Merry Christmas."

Amber, Lance, Zoe and Aaron pulled up with their kids in tow. Becca drew in a deep breath and felt tears prick her eyes. She was grateful. So very grateful to be alive and in this place at this moment.

"Come on," Nathan said. "I'm hungry and I'm terrified your dad is going to eat all the pie." He took her hand and pulled her to the door.

Only to meet Seth and Tonya coming back out. Tonya looking pained and Seth appearing scared to death. "What's going on?" Becca asked.

"She's not going to make it through lunch," Seth said. "She didn't bother to tell me she's been having contractions all morning."

"The truck, Seth," Tonya said through gritted teeth. "Get the truck. Please."

Without another word, Seth darted for the vehicle. Becca took her cousin's hand. "How far apart?"

"Well, they were fifteen minutes apart earlier this morning and up until we left to come over so I didn't think much about it, but the last three have been four minutes apart, so I think it's best to head to the hospital especially since they seem to be coming early."

"We'll go with you."

Tonya squeezed her eyes shut and with Nathan and Becca's help, sank onto the porch step. Becca helped her breath through another contraction. When Tonya opened her eyes, tears glittered there. "It's time. I'm going to meet them today."

"What are you naming them?"

"Thomas Lane and Shelby Elizabeth."

"Beautiful names for beautiful babies."

Seth pulled to a stop, and Nathan held the door while Seth rushed out to help Tonya into the passenger seat. "We'll be there soon," Becca said.

"No. Enjoy the meal. Come later when you'll be able to hold them. They'll probably be in the NICU a couple of weeks so there will be time."

Nathan nodded. "Okay. Send us updates."

"We will."

Seth took off and Nathan grabbed her in a hug. "Let's eat. I have a feeling it's going to be a crazy day."

"A wonderful, beautiful, exciting day. New beginnings and new life. It doesn't get any better than that."

Together, they walked back toward the house. Toward a future filled with love no matter what life might throw at them. Becca sighed with contentment and knew that while some memories faded or got lost in the midst of a traumatic event, this was one day she'd never forget for as long as she lived.

* * * * *

If you enjoyed CHRISTMAS RANCH RESCUE,
look for these other books in the
WRANGLER'S CORNER *series:*

THE LAWMAN RETURNS
RODEO RESCUER
PROTECTING HER DAUGHTER
CLASSIFIED CHRISTMAS MISSION

Dear Reader,

Thanks so much for coming back to Wrangler's Corner with Becca and Nathan's story. They've become two of my favorite characters. Probably because I got to work on this story with my favorite daughter. Okay, my only daughter, but she's still my favorite. This was truly a very special story for me because we brainstormed it together. When the Killer Voices contest was announced, Lauryn (then fifteen years old) decided she wanted to give it a try. She came up with the characters and wrote the first page to be submitted. Of course I helped her out by telling her what to include in the first page, like a lot of suspense, and she took it from there. She based Becca's character on her own experience with a fall from a horse and the misery of a sprained back and a concussion. She then added her years of experience riding horses (since she was about four years old) and voilà, had a great heroine for the story. I came up with the hero for the most part, and then she and I brainstormed how the story should unfold. Lauryn then wrote the next two chapters, which I helped her edit, and she went through to the last round of the contest, where she was asked to submit a full manuscript. Well, her schedule was such that there was no way she was going to be able to do it. Exams in May, then a very busy summer with mission trips and so on. So, the story was shelved. About six months or so ago, I asked her if she was ever going to finish the story and she said, "No, probably not, but you can if you want to."

And so I did. I tweaked it a bit to make it fit the Wrangler's Corner series, but I felt she deserved her name on the cover due to all the initial hard work she put into it. We hope you love Becca and Nathan's story as much as we do! Have a blessed Christmas and very happy New Year. May you never run out of books to read!

Much love and blessings,
Lynette

Dear Reader,

This book was originally supposed to be entered into the Killer Voices contest back in 2014. I started working on it at the beach during spring break of my sophomore year of high school because it was too cold and rainy to go out and do anything. I intended to just write and enter the contest for pleasure, but the Lord obviously had other plans. I sent my mom the first chapter, and she encouraged me to keep writing, so I did. Brainstorming with her for the rest of the book was fun because she is so passionate about writing and gets excited about the characters and story line. She's the most creative person I know (which was annoying in high school when I wanted to stay out late with friends and she was worried I was going to end up kidnapped at gunpoint), but if it wasn't for her encouragement, the chapters and ideas probably would have wound up being deleted and that would have been the end of it all. I did learn that while writing fiction can be fun, it is also very difficult. Writers have my full admiration and appreciation. And while working on this story with my mother was fun, it looks like I'm going to be transferring my writing to everything that comes with law school. Maybe I'll write a book again one day, but for now, I'm just so proud to say that I got to work on this project with her (even though she did most of the work). I hope you all enjoyed the story!

God Bless!
Lauryn Eason

Get 2 Free Books,

<u>Plus</u> 2 Free Gifts—

just for trying the Reader Service!

Suddenly, Macy stood. "Do you smell that, Tanner?"

Smoke. There was a fire somewhere. Close.

"Go get Addie," he barked. "Now!"

Macy flew up the steps, urgency nipping at her heels.

Where there was smoke, there was fire. Wasn't that the saying?

Somehow, she instinctively knew that those words were the truth. Whoever had set this fire had done it on purpose. They wanted to push Tanner, Macy and Addie outside. Into harm. Into a trap.

As she climbed higher, she spotted the flames. They licked the edges of the house, already beginning to consume it.

Despite the heat around her, ice formed in her gut.

She scooped up Addie, hating to wake the infant when she was sleeping so peacefully.

Macy had to move fast.

She rushed downstairs, where Tanner waited for her. He grabbed her arm and ushered her toward the door.

Flames licked the walls now, slowly devouring the house. Tanner pulled out his gun and turned toward Macy.

She could hardly breathe. Just then, Addie awoke with a cry.

The poor baby. She had no idea what was going on. She didn't deserve this.

Tanner kept his arm around her and Addie.

"Let's do this," he said. His voice held no room for argument.

He opened the door. Flames licked their way inside.

Macy gasped as the edges of the fire felt dangerously close. She pulled Addie tightly to her chest, determined to protect the baby at all costs.

She held her breath as they slipped outside and rushed to the car. There was no car seat. There hadn't been time.

Instead, Macy continued to hold Addie close to her chest, trying to shield her from any incoming danger or threats. She lifted a quick prayer.

Please help us.

As Tanner started the car, a bullet shattered the window.

Don't miss
THE BABY ASSIGNMENT by Christy Barritt,
available January 2018 wherever
Love Inspired® Suspense books and ebooks are sold.

www.LoveInspired.com

Love Inspired®

Inspirational Romance to
Warm Your Heart and Soul

Join our social communities to connect
with other readers who share your love!

Sign up for the Love Inspired newsletter
at **www.LoveInspired.com** to be the
first to find out about upcoming titles,
special promotions and exclusive content.

CONNECT WITH US AT:

Harlequin.com/Community

 Facebook.com/LoveInspiredBooks

 Twitter.com/LoveInspiredBks

LISOCIAL2017

Jeremiah looked up to see a ladder wobbling. A dark-haired woman stood at the very top, her arms windmilling.

He leaped into the small room as she fell. After years of being tossed shocks of corn and hay bales, he caught her easily. He jumped out of the way, holding her to him as the ladder crashed to the linoleum floor.

"Are you okay?" he asked. His heart had slammed against his chest when he saw her teetering.

"I'm fine."

"Who are you?" he asked at the same time she did.

"I'm Jeremiah Stoltzfus," he answered. "You are…?"

"Mercy Bamberger."

"Bamberger? Like Rudy Bamberger?"

"Yes. Do you know my grandfather?"

Well, that explained who she was and why she was in the house.

"He invited me to come and look around."

She shook her head. "I don't understand why."

"Didn't he tell you he's selling me his farm?"

"No!"

"I'm sorry to take you by surprise," he said gently, "but I'll be closing the day after tomorrow."

"Impossible! The farm's not for sale."

"Why don't you get your *grossdawdi*, and we'll settle this?"

"I can't."

"Why not?"

She blinked back sudden tears. "Because he's dead."

"Rudy is dead?"

"Yes. It was a massive heart attack. He was buried the day before yesterday."

"I'm sorry," Jeremiah said with sincerity.

"Grandpa Rudy told me the farm would be mine after he passed away."

"Then why would he sign a purchase agreement with me?"

"But my grandfather died," she whispered. "Doesn't that change things?"

"I don't know. I'm not sure what we should do," he said.

"Me, either. However, you need to know I'm not going to relinquish my family's farm to you or anyone else."

"But—"

"We moved in a couple of days ago. We're not giving it up." She crossed her arms over her chest. "It's our home."

Don't miss
AN AMISH ARRANGEMENT
by Jo Ann Brown, available January 2018 wherever
Love Inspired® books and ebooks are sold.

www.LoveInspired.com